DEATH BY THE BOOK

A POISON INK MYSTERY

BETH BYERS

If there's anything I love, it's a good author with a large catalogue.

With much love to those writers who went before and inspire my every day:

Georgette Heyer, Dorothy L. Sayers, Ngaio Marsh,
D.E. Stevenson, and hundreds more.

AUTHOR'S NOTE

This book was inspired by the books of the past. I wondered how fun it would be to throw in a murder for those small towns like Barsetshire for Anthony Trollope or Miss Buncle's Book by DE Stevenson. I was in love with the crazy scenes Georgette Heyer puts together when all goes mad. I wanted to play with multiple perspectives like Anthony Trollope does in his Barsetshire Chronicles and Elizabeth Crawford does in Cranford and even J.K. Rowling does in The Casual Vacancy.

This author always recommends those books over her own, with particular love for the authors listed above. They are, and always have been, my favorite writers. There are reasons that they are the greats of their age, and I am in awe of their brilliance.

CHAPTER 1

GEORGETTE MARSH

eorgette Dorothy Marsh stared at the statement from her bank with a dawning horror. The dividends had been falling, but this…this wasn't livable. She bit down on the inside of her lip and swallowed frantically. *What was she going to do?* Tears were burning in the back of her eyes, and her heart was racing frantically.

There wasn't enough for—for—anything. Not for cream for her tea or resoling her shoes or firewood for the winter. Georgette glanced out the window, remembered it was spring, and realized that something must be done.

Something, but *what?*

"Miss?" Eunice said from the doorway, "the tea at Mrs. Wilkes is this afternoon. You asked me to remind you."

Georgette nodded, frantically trying to hide her tears from her maid, but the servant had known Georgette since the day of her birth, caring for her from her infancy to the current day.

"What has happened?"

"The…the dividends," Georgette breathed. She didn't have enough air to speak clearly. "The dividends. It's not enough."

Eunice's head cocked as she examined her mistress and then she said, "Something must be done."

"But what?" Georgette asked, biting down on her lip again. *Hard.*

CHARLES AARON

"Uncle?"

Charles Aaron glanced up from the stack of papers on his desk at his nephew some weeks after Georgette Marsh had written her book in a fury of desperation. It was Robert Aaron who had discovered the book, and it was Charles Aaron who would give it life.

Robert had been working at Aaron & Luther Publishing House for a year before Georgette's book appeared in the mail, and he read the slush pile of books that were submitted by new authors before either of the partners stepped in. It was an excellent rewarding work when you found that one book that separated itself from the pile, and Robert got that thrill of excitement every time he found a book that had a touch of *something*. It was the very feeling that had Charles himself pursuing a career in publishing and eventually creating his own firm.

It didn't seem to matter that Charles had his long history of discovering authors and their books. Familiarity had most definitely *not* led to contempt. He was, he had to admit, in love with reading— fiction especially—and the creative mind. He had learned that some of the books he found would speak only to him.

Often, however, some he loved would become best sellers. With the best sellers, Charles felt he was sharing a delightful secret with the world. There was magic in discovering a new writer. A contagious sort of magic that had infected Robert. There was nothing that Charles enjoyed more than hearing someone recommend a book he'd published to another.

"You've found something?"

Robert shrugged, but he also handed the manuscript over a smile right on the edge of his lips and shining eyes that flicked to the manuscript over and over again. "Yes, I think so." He wasn't confident enough yet to feel certain, but Charles had noticed for some time that Robert was getting closer and closer to no longer needing anyone to guide him.

"I'll look it over soon."

It was the end of the day and Charles had a headache building behind his eyes. He always did on the days when he had to deal with the bestseller Thomas Spencer. He was too successful for his own good and expected any publishing company to bend entirely to his will.

Robert watched Charles load the manuscript into his satchel, bouncing just a little before he pulled back and cleared his throat. The boy—man, Charles supposed—smoothed his suit, flashed a grin, and left the office. Leaving for the day wasn't a bad plan. He took his satchel and—as usual—had dinner at his club before retiring to a corner of the room with an overstuffed armchair, an Old-Fashioned, and his pipe.

Charles glanced around the club, noting the other regulars. Most of them were bachelors who found it easier to eat at the club than to employ a cook. Every once in a while there was a family man who'd escaped the house for an evening with the gents, but for the most part —it was bachelors like himself.

When Charles opened the neat pages of 'Joseph Jones's *The Chronicles of Harper's Bend,* he intended to read only a small portion of the book. To get a feel for what Robert had seen and perhaps determine whether it was worth a more thorough look. After a few pages, Charles decided upon just a few more. A few more pages after that, and he left his club to return home and finish the book by his own fire.

It might have been early summer, but they were also in the middle of a ferocious storm. Charles preferred the crackle of fire wherever possible when he read, as well as a good cup of tea. There was no question that the book was well done. There was no question that Charles would be contacting the author and making an offer on the book. *The Chronicles of Harper's Bend* was, in fact, so captivating in its honesty, he couldn't quite decide whether this author loved the small towns of England or despised them. He rather felt it might be both.

Either way, it was quietly sarcastic and so true to the little village that raised Charles Aaron that he felt he might turn the page and discover the old woman who'd lived next door to his parents or the vicar of the church he'd attended as a boy. Charles felt as though he knew the people stepping off the pages.

Yes, Charles thought, yes. This one, he thought, *this* would be a best seller. Charles could feel it in his bones. He tapped out his pipe into the ashtray. This would be one of those books he looked back on with pride at having been the first to know that this book was the next big thing. Despite the lateness of the hour, Charles approached his bedroom with an energized delight. A letter would be going out in the morning.

~

GEORGETTE MARSH

It was on the very night that Charles read the *Chronicles* that Miss Georgette Dorothy Marsh paced, once again, in front of her fireplace. The wind whipped through the town of Bard's Crook sending a flurry of leaves swirling around the graves in the small churchyard and then shooing them down to a small lane off of High Street where the elderly Mrs. Henry Parker had been awake for some time. She had woken worried over her granddaughter who was recovering too slowly from the measles.

The wind rushed through the cottages at the end of the lane, causing the gate at the Wilkes house to rattle. Dr. Wilkes and his wife were curled up together in their bed sharing warmth in the face of the changing weather. A couple much in love, snuggling into their beds on a windy evening was a joy for them both.

The leaves settled into a pile in the corner of the picket fence right at the very last cottage on that lane of Miss Georgette Dorothy Marsh. Throughout most of Bard's Crook, people were sleeping. Their hot water bottles were at the ends of their beds, their blankets were piled high, and they went to bed prepared for another day. The unseasonable chill had more than one household enjoying a warm cup of milk at bedtime, though not Miss Marsh's economizing household.

Miss Marsh, unlike the others, was not asleep. She didn't have a fire as she was quite at the end of her income and every adjustment must be made. If she were going to be honest with herself, and she very much didn't want to be—she was past the end of her income. Her account had become overdraft, her dividends had dried up, and it might be time to recognize that her last-ditch effort of writing a book about her neighbors had not been successful.

She had looked at the lives of folks like Anthony Trollope who both worked and wrote novels and Louisa May Alcott who wrote to relieve the stress of her life and to help bring in financial help. As much as Georgette loved to read, and she did, she loved the idea that somewhere out there an author was using their art to restart their lives. There was a romance to being a writer, but she wondered just how many writers were pragmatic behind the fairytales they crafted. It wasn't, Georgette thought, going to be her story like Louisa May Alcott. Georgette was going to do something else.

"Miss Georgie," Eunice said, "I can hear you. You'll catch something dreadful if you don't sleep." The sound of muttering chased Georgie, who had little doubt Eunice was complaining about catching something dreadful herself.

"I'm sorry, Eunice," Georgie called. "I—" Georgie opened the door to her bedroom and faced the woman. She had worked for Mr. and Mrs. Marsh when Georgie had been born and in all the years of loss and change, Eunice had never left Georgie. Even now when the economies made them both uncomfortable. "Perhaps—"

"It'll be all right in the end, Miss Georgie. Now to bed with you."

Georgette did not, however, go to bed. Instead, she pulled out her pen and paper and listed all of the things she might do to further economize. They had a kitchen garden already, and it provided the vast majority of what they ate. They did their own mending and did not buy new clothes. They had one goat that they milked and made their own cheese. Though Georgette had to recognize that she rather feared goats. They were, of all creatures, devils. They would just randomly knock one over.

Georgie shivered and refused to consider further goats. Perhaps she could tutor someone? She thought about those she knew and realized that no one in Bard's Crook would hire the quiet Georgette Dorothy Marsh to influence their children. The village's wallflower and cipher? Hardly a legitimate option for any caring parent. Georgette was all too aware of what her neighbors thought of her. She rose again, pacing more quietly as she considered and rejected her options.

Georgie paced until quite late and then sat down with her pen and paper and wondered if she should try again with her writing. Something else. Something with more imagination. She had started her book with fits until she'd landed on practicing writing by describing an episode of her village. It had grown into something more, something beyond Bard's Crook with just conclusions to the lives she saw around her.

When she'd started *The Chronicles of Harper's Bend*, she had been more desperate than desirous of a career in writing. Once again, she recognized that she must do something and she wasn't well-suited to anything but writing. There were no typist jobs in Bard's Crook, no secretarial work. The time when rich men paid for companions for their wives or elderly mothers was over, and the whole of the world was struggling to survive, Georgette included.

She'd thought of going to London for work, but if she left her snug little cottage, she'd have to pay for lodging elsewhere. Georgie sighed into her palm and then went to bed. There was little else to do at that moment. Something, however, must be done.

CHAPTER 2

$\mathcal{T}$hree days later, the day dawned with a return to summer, and the hills were rolling out from Bard's Crook as though being whispered over by the gods themselves. It seemed all too possible that Aurora had descended from Olympus to smile on the village. Miss Marsh's solitary hen with her cold, hard eyes was click-clacking around the garden, eating her seeds, and generally disgusting the lady of the house.

Miss Marsh had woken to the sound of the newspaper boy arriving, but she had dressed rather leisurely. There was little to look forward to outside of a good cup of tea, light on the sugar, and without cream. She told herself she preferred her tea without cream, but in the quiet of her bedroom, she could admit that she very much wanted cream in her tea. If Georgie could persuade a god to her door, it would be the goddess Fortuna to bless Georgie's book and provide enough ready money to afford cream and better teas. Was her life even worth living with the watered-down muck she'd been forced to drink lately?

Georgette put on her dress, which had been old when it had been given to her and was the perfect personification of dowdiness. She might also add to her dream list, enough money for a dress or two. By

Jove, she thought, how wonderful would a hat be? A lovely new one? Or perhaps a coat that fit her? The list of things that needed to be replaced in her life was near endless.

She sighed into the mirror glancing over her familiar face with little emotion. She neither liked nor disliked her face. She knew her hair was pretty enough though it tended towards a frizziness she'd never learned to anticipate or tame. The color was a decent medium brown with corresponding medium brown eyes. Her skin was clear of blemishes, for which she was grateful, though she despised the freckles that sprinkled over her nose and cheeks. Her dress rose to her collar, but her freckles continued down her arms and over her chest. At least her lips were perfectly adequate, neither thin nor full, but nothing to cause a second glance. Like all of her, she thought, there was nothing to cause a second glance.

Despite her lackluster looks, she didn't despise her face. She rather liked herself. Unlike many she knew, the inside of her head was not a terrible place to be. She had no major regrets and enjoyed her own humor well enough even if she rarely bothered to share her thoughts with others.

Georgette supposed if she had been blessed with liveliness, she might be rather pretty, but she knew herself well. She was quiet. Both in her persona and voice, and she was easily ignored. It had never been something that she bemoaned. She was who she was and though very few knew her well, those who knew her liked her. Those who knew her well—the very few who could claim such a status—liked her very well.

On a morning when Georgie was not worrying over her bank account, she could be counted on entering the dining room at 9:00 a.m. On that morning, however, she was rather late. She considered goats again as she brushed her teeth—no one else in Bard's Crook kept goats though there were several who kept cows. Those bedamned goats kept coming back to her mind, but she'd rather sell everything she owned and throw herself on the mercy of the city than keep goats. She had considered trying to sew clothing while she'd pulled on her stockings and slipped her shoes on her feet. She had considered whether she might make hats when she'd brushed her hair, and she had wondered if she might take a lodger as she'd straightened her dress and exited her bedroom.

All of her options were rejected before she reached the base of her stairs, and she entered the dining room with an edge of desperation. As she took her seat at the head of the table and added a very small amount of sugar to her weak tea, her attention was caught by the most unexpected of sights. A letter to the left of her plate. Georgette lifted it with shaking hands and read the return address. Aaron & Luther Publishing. She gasped and then slowly blew out the air.

"Be brave, dear girl," she whispered, as she cut open the envelope. "If they say no, you can always send your book to Anderson Books. Hope is not gone. Not yet."

She pulled the single sheet of paper out and wondered if it was a good sign or a bad sign that they had not returned her book. Slowly, carefully, she unfolded the letter, her tea and toast entirely abandoned as she read the contents.

Moments later, the letter fluttered down to her plate and she sipped her scalding hot tea and didn't notice the burn.

"Is all well, Miss Georgie?" The maid was standing in the doorway. Her wrinkled face was fixated on her girl with the same tense anticipation that had Georgette reading her letter over and over while it lay open on her plate. Those dark eyes were fixated on Georgette's face with careful concern.

"I need cream, Eunice." Georgette nodded to her maid. "We're saved. They want *Chronicles*. My goodness, my *dear, wonderful* woman, see to the cream and let's stop making such weak tea until we discover the details of the fiscal benefits."

Eunice had to have been as relieved as Georgette, but the maid simply nodded stalwartly and came back into the dining room a few minutes later with a fresh pot of strong tea, a full bowl of sugar, and the cream that had been intended for supper. It was still the cheapest tea that was sold in Bard's Crook, but it was black and strong and tasted rather like nirvana on her tongue when Georgette drank it down.

"I'll go up to London tomorrow. He wants to see me in the afternoon, but he states very clearly he wants the book. We're saved."

"Don't count your chickens before they hatch, Miss Georgie."

"By Jove, we aren't just saved from a lack of cream, Eunice. We're saved from goats! We're saved my dear. Have a seat and enjoy a cuppa yourself."

Eunice clucked and returned to the kitchen instead. They might be saved, but the drawing room still needed to be done, dinner still needed to be started, and the laundry and mending were waiting for no woman.

WHEN MISS MARSH made her way into London the following day, she was wearing her old cloche, which was quite dingy but the best she had, a coat that was worn at the cuffs and the hem, and shoes that were just starting to have a hole worn into the bottom. Perhaps, she thought, there would even be enough to re-sole her shoes.

On the train into London from Bard's Crook, only Mr. Thornton was taking the train from the village. When he inquired after her business, she quite shocked herself when she made up a story about meeting an old Scottish school chum for tea. Mr. Thornton admitted he intended to meet with his lawyer. He was rather notorious in Bard's Crook for changing his will as often as the wind changed direction. An event he always announced with an air of doom and a frantic waggling of his eyebrows.

Mr. Thornton had married a woman from the factories who refused to acknowledge her past, and together they had three children. Those children—now adults—included two rebellious sons and one clinging daughter. He also had quite a slew of righteous nephews who deserved the acclaim they received. Whenever his wife bullied him too hard or his sons rebelled too overtly, the will altered in favor of the righteous nephews until such time as an appropriate repentance could be made.

Georgie had long since taken to watching the flip-flopping of the will with a delighted air. As far as she could tell, no one but herself enjoyed the changing of his will, but enjoying things that others didn't seem to notice had long been her fate.

The fortunate news of the inheritance situation was that Mr. Thornton's nephews were unaware of the changing of their fortunes. The clinging daughter's fortune was set in stone. She never rebelled and thus never had her fortunes reversed, but she clung rather too fiercely to be a favored inheritor.

Mr. Thornton handed Miss Marsh down from the train, offered to share a black cab, and then left her without regret when she made a weak excuse. Miss Marsh selected her own black cab, cutting into her ready money dreadfully, and hoped that whatever occurred today would restore her cash in hand.

~

CHARLES AARON

"Mr. Aaron," Schmidt said, "your afternoon appointment has arrived."

"Wonderful," Charles replied. "Send him in with tea, will you Schmidtty?"

"Her, sir."

"Her? Isn't my appointment with an author?" Charles felt a flash of irritation. He was very much looking forward to meeting the author of *The Chronicles of Harper's Bend.* He had, in fact, read the book twice more since that first time.

Schmidt's lips twitched when he said, "It seems the author is a Miss Marsh."

Charles thought over the book and realized that of course Mr. Jones was a Miss Marsh. Who but a woman would realize the fierce shame of bribing one's children with candies to behave for church? Charles could almost hear the tirade of his grandmother about the lack of mothering skills in the upcoming generations.

"Well, send her in, and tea as well." Charles rubbed his hands together in glee. He did adore meeting new writers. They were never what you expected, but they all had one thing in common. Behind their dull or beautiful faces, behind their polite smiles and small talk, there were whole worlds. Characters with secrets that only the writer knew. Unnecessary histories that were cut viciously from the story and hidden away only to be known by the author.

Charles rather enjoyed asking the writers random questions about their characters' secret histories. Tell me, author, Charles would say, as they shared a cup of tea or a pipe, what does so-and-so do on Christmas morning? Or what is his/her favorite color? He loved when they answered readily, knowing that of course so-and-so woke early on Christmas morning, opened presents and had a rather spectacular full English only to sleep it off on the Chesterfield near the fire.

He loved it when they described what they ate down to the nearest detail as though the character's traditional breakfast had been made since time immemorial rather than born with a pen and hidden behind the gaze of the person with whom Charles was sharing an hour or two.

Charles had long since become inured to the varying attitudes of authors. Thomas Spencer, who had given Charles a rather terrible headache that had been cured by Miss Marsh's delightful book, wore dandified clothes and had an arrogant air. Spencer felt the cleverness of his books justified his rudeness.

On the other hand, an even more brilliant writer, Henry Moore, was a little man with a large stomach. He kept a half-dozen cats, spoiled his children terribly, and was utterly devoted to his wife. In a gathering of authors, Moore would be the most successful and the cleverest by far but be overshadowed by every other writer in attendance.

Miss Marsh, Charles saw, fell into the 'Moore' category. She seemed as timid as a newborn rabbit as she edged into his office. Her gaze flit about, taking in the stack of manuscripts, the shelf of books he'd published over the course of his career, the windows that looked onto a dingy alleyway, and the large wooden desk.

She was, he thought, a dowdy little thing. Her eyes were nice enough, but they barely met his own, and she didn't seem to know quite what to say. Her freckles seemed to be rather spectacular—if one liked freckles—but it was hard to know anything with her timid movements. Especially with her face barely meeting his own. That was all right, he thought, he'd done this many times, and she was very new to the selling of a book and the signing of contracts.

"Hello," he said rather cheerily, hoping that his tone would set her at ease.

She glanced up at him and then back down, her gaze darting around his office again. Mr. Aaron wondered just what she was seeing amidst all of his things. He wouldn't be surprised to find she was noting things that the average fellow would overlook.

"Would you like tea?"

Miss Marsh nodded, and he poured her a cup to which she added a hefty amount of cream and sugar. He grinned at the sight of her milky tea and then leaned back as she slowly spun her teacup on the saucer.

"Why Joseph Jones? Why a pen name at all?"

Miss Marsh blinked rather rapidly and then admitted, "Well..." Her gaze darted to the side, and she said, "I was rather inspired by my neighbors, but I would prefer to avoid their gossip as well. Can you imagine?" A cheeky grin crossed her face for a moment, and he was entranced. "If they discovered that Antoinette Moore wrote a book?"

"Is that you?"

"Pieces of her," she admitted, and he frowned. The quiet woman in front of him certainly had the mannerisms of the character, but he couldn't quite see Miss Moore writing a book and sending it off. She was such an innocuous, almost unnecessary character in the book.

Was Miss Marsh a literary portraitist? He grinned at the idea and wanted nothing more than to visit Harper's Bend or wherever it was that this realistic portrayal existed in real life. What he would give to have an afternoon tea with the likes of Mrs. Morton and her ilk.

Mr. Aaron glanced over Miss Marsh. Her old cloche and worn coat were not lost on him, and he supposed if he'd met her anywhere else he'd never have looked at her twice. Having read her book, however, he suddenly felt as though she were far more charming than she'd otherwise have been.

Her gaze, with ordinary medium brown eyes, seemed to have untold depths, and her freckles seemed to be an outward indicator of a woman who could look at her village and turn it into a witty caricature, acting as a warning that this was a woman who said nothing and noticed everything.

He grinned at her. "I read your book, and I liked it."

Her eyes flashed and a bright grin crossed her face, and he realized she was a little prettier than he'd noticed. It was that shocked delight on her face that made him add, "I like it quite well indeed."

Miss Marsh clasped her hands tightly together, and Mr. Aaron did not miss how her grip camouflaged the trembling of her hands.

"Tell me about it," he said kindly. "Why did you write it? This is a portrait of your neighbors?"

It was the kindness that got Miss Marsh to open up, and then she couldn't seem to stem the tide of her thoughts; they sped out. "Well, it was my dividends you see. They've quite dried up. I was struggling before, but they'd always come in and then they didn't, and I was quite —" Miss Marsh trailed off and Mr. Aaron could imagine the situation all too easily. "at my wit's end. Only then I thought of Louisa May Alcott and the other lady writers, and I thought I might as well try as not."

The world was struggling and Miss Marsh, who may have escaped the early failing of things, had eventually succumbed as so many had. As she said, her dividends had dried up. He could imagine her lying awake worried and uncertain or perhaps pacing her home. There was something so unpretentious about her revelation that Mr. Aaron was even more charmed. She'd come to the end of things, and she'd turned that worry into the most charming of stories. Not just a charming story, but one filled with heart and delight in the little things. He liked her all the better for it.

CHAPTER 3

*W*hen Mr. Aaron brought the contract for Miss Marsh to sign, she didn't ask any questions as she read and signed. He watched her in utter consternation, thinking she very much needed a protector. He admitted the contract *was* fair, but did she know it was fair? Or was she just trusting him? She glanced up at him with those sweet, honey brown eyes and felt certain she was trusting him. His gaze focused on her again. Her pale skin with the freckles, the sweet gaze, the hidden cleverness. She seemed a puzzle that only he had solved.

"Did you want to take the contract and talk with someone about it?"

She shook her head.

It was a fair contract, perhaps more generous than a new writer with no history deserved, but he felt confident that her book would do well, and he wanted to cultivate her trust. Loyal, talented authors who didn't change their publishers as often as they changed their shoes were the backbone of publishing companies like Aaron & Luther. He suspected that Miss Marsh would be utterly loyal to his company as long as he was fair.

"Miss Marsh, I—"

That cheeky grin crossed her face again, and she admitted, "I would sell it to you if it were unfair, Mr. Aaron. I am rather at the end of things. It is fair, isn't it?" Those medium brown eyes crossed his face once again, and he felt that even if hadn't been fair, he would have changed it in that moment just to make it so.

He nodded once, and she smiled that cheeky grin at him catching at his imagination more thoroughly than even his book.

Miss Marsh signed with a neat signature and accepted the cheque with bright eyes that told him she was desperate for money even if she hadn't admitted it to him. He felt both understanding and sympathy when she rapidly blinked away the shine from her eyes. Times were hard and more than one business or family or person had gone from comfortable to ruined. He had walked the edge more than he'd like with his company, but he'd been fortunate to have a few successful authors who were as loyal as he hoped Miss Marsh would be.

"This is the beginning of something lucrative for us both, I think," he told her, but she didn't believe him. Her gaze flicked to his face, doubt evident, and then quickly to the side to hide those thoughts of hers.

If she wrote about her neighbors, then Robert and himself were the only people to have read her book. She wouldn't have received the praise of a good friend or a well-trusted neighbor like so many did before they sent their books off, so she may well be entirely unaware of what a good book she'd written. She'd learn that he wasn't playing with her emotions when she saw the sales and the reviews come in. "I look forward to what you write next."

"Oh," Miss Marsh breathed, looking shocked at the idea. "Another book?"

He grinned at her and gave her a wink. He'd learned long ago the power of ready money to persuade an author to write. The first books were written out of a nebulous desire to accomplish a life-long goal or perhaps, like with Miss Marsh, the need for money. Once authors realized what they had done, they often ended up in a surreal haze of delight where they could do things like afford a new coat. Something he hoped Miss Marsh would do for herself, along with a new hat.

Once the author's basic needs were met, the idea of perhaps having new shoes or even a trip to the seashore persuaded them to return to their pen and paper and craft another story. Somewhere along the way—writing became their life and story ideas abounded, too many to ever write. Charles Aaron had very little concern that he would not see another story from Miss Marsh, although, he wanted it already. He'd found his mind returning to the story she'd crafted. He wanted more—which was how he always knew when he had a winner.

"Write me another book, please?"

Her head cocked and she examined him as if he were a very strange sort of creature?

"Another book?"

"Please."

"For this much again?"

"Perhaps even more if the book does as well as I expect."

Her gaze widened and she asked, "But what shall I write?"

"Throw someone else into your little town and cause trouble."

She frowned a little and then said, "Well…I suppose I could do it once more."

"I would be ever so delighted to see what happens with Miss Moore next," Charles told her and then realized he was very, very curious about what would happen next with Miss Marsh.

Charles saw Miss Marsh out and regretted when she left. There was something about the way she took in the world around her. He felt as though she was seeing things that he wasn't. It was probably why her book was so clever.

Normally he'd have stopped at the doorway to his office, but he ended up seeing her down the stairs and hailing a black cab for her. She seemed dazed when she left. This was a book he'd hurry to print, he thought. The perfect lightness for the autumn. The rains would come, the clouds would cover the sky, and readers would be able to curl up into the cheery brightness of Miss Marsh's little book.

GEORGETTE MARSH

Miss Marsh sat back in the black cab as the man asked, "Where to, ma'am?"

She flinched a little at the ma'am. She was only twenty-seven years old. She supposed that if it were Jane Austen's time, she'd be the dowdy woman who had long since given up hope of marrying. She'd be...yes, Charlotte Lucas. Georgette was the somewhat clever friend who succumbed to the advances of the horrible Mr. Collins by telling herself that she was not romantic.

A moment later, Georgette gave the cabbie the location of a bank. He didn't note the sudden brightness in her eyes. It wasn't present in her soft voice as she arranged for him to wait for her while she deposited the cheque into her account. The overdraft would be resolved and cream would be a ready thing again.

No, she thought, as she walked out of the bank with a new lightness of step. Across the street was a little teashop, and Georgette's eyes brightened with avarice. No, not Charlotte, Georgette told herself as she hurried between the cars and darted inside. She was going to splurge on tea, and it was going to be wonderful. As she ordered the best of English breakfast tea, a delightful herbal mixture for the evening that smelled of oranges and spice along with some Chinese blends, Georgette's mind returned to Charlotte Lucas.

Not Charlotte, Georgette told herself. Charlotte had given in to the fate placed before her, and Georgette had found another way. She had *published a book!* She had resolved her failing dividends and reset her monies. She had...self-knowing struck Georgette...she was, she thought, a Charlotte after all. If Mr. Collins had offered Georgette a saving hand, she'd have accepted his rescue. The difference between Charlotte Lucas and Georgette Marsh was that no Mr. Collins had come at just the right moment.

Her pride was gone again as she returned to the black cab and had him take her to the train station. Mr. Thornton was not returning on the same train, so Georgette could stare out the window and watch the day roll by and her village appear.

When she walked down the street, her secret was bright in her eyes and her spirit, but no one noticed. Mrs. Thornton, the will-changer's wife, nodded to Georgette and she passed by in her motor-car. Dr. Wilkes waved a cheery hello and asked Georgette how she was, but hurried without listening to the answer. She didn't take it personally; she noted his doctor's satchel and the dark circles under his eyes. She'd heard that the Smith children had the measles and that Mr. Nyman was doing poorly. She was happy, in fact, to see Dr. Wilkes had pushed his glasses up on his head. He glanced up as he hurriedly moved down the street, closing his eyes and soaking in what sunshine was possible.

Towards the wood at the end of the lane, the soft and sweet Eliza Evans ushered her silent little girls towards the trees where she'd try and fail to get them to play happily. They each carried dolls that looked as new and perfect as they were the day they were given to the little girls.

The doctor's wife, Mrs. Wilkes, met Mrs. Evans as they entered the wood. The Wilkes boys were wild and dirty, and they raced ahead of the Evans girls who flinched as the boys passed, but Georgette noted how the little girls' heads turned following the whooping boys.

With her book on her mind and the sight of those poor children in her gaze, Georgette recalled the scandalous ending that Georgette had given Mrs. Evans in the book. How Georgette wished that any possible variation of escape were possible for Mrs. Evans.

It was funny what you did when you could hide behind the name of a pen name, Georgette thought, knowing that much of the village would be horrified to know of what Georgette had envisioned. She waved when Mrs. Wilkes turned back and saw her, but the secret author carried on. She wasn't sure she should trust herself around anyone else until her news was settled and her tongue was firmly behind her teeth.

She glanced down at her luxurious package. The tea would be for her and Eunice alone. Like Mrs. Thornton, Georgette would only serve the worst tea when guests arrived. She grinned wickedly at the thought. She had squirreled away money in a box inside of her wardrobe. Now that her account was going to be positive, she felt certain that she and Eunice should celebrate. What else besides tea?

Chocolates? Perhaps a cake from the bakery? Yes, that. Georgette stopped beside the bakery and made her way in. Mrs. Hannigan had a small butter cake, swathed in chocolate frosting, and Georgette requested it.

"Celebrating?" Mrs. Hannigan asked.

"Oh, Mrs. Hannigan," Georgette said, "I fear it is more a bit of a hankering that has won out over my sensibility."

Mrs. Hannigan gave Georgette a look that told her that she should consider a bit more frugality. Georgette glanced to the ground and waited as Mrs. Hannigan wrapped up the cake to be taken home. She wished the baker a merry day and then resolved to drink tea, heavy on the cream, eat cake for supper and overindulge until her stomach ached and she wanted to do nothing but sleep. She might just sleep, she thought, curled onto the sofa. Though, it had been purchased by Georgette's grandmother when she'd married, and the days of it being comfortable to sleep on or even sit on were long since past.

How much would a new sofa set her back? Perhaps a nice over-sized Chesterfield and large armchairs? Georgette took a few minutes to dream of it and then she thought about the book she had written. The first half of it was something of a history of her village. There was a point, however, where Georgette had started to give her neighbors stories beyond reality. Could she do it again? Perhaps entirely fiction-ally this time?

She arrived home and placed the cake on the table near the door. She would have told Mr. Aaron that she had very little imagination earlier that day. As she considered the empty fireplace in her parlor, Georgette had a flash of sheer, unadulterated dreaming and pulled a piece of paper from the roll-top desk in the corner of her parlor. She pulled out a fountain pen and wrote out a list of things that needed updating in her home and how many books it would take her to reach that goal.

The number was a little terrifying, she thought. Mr. Aaron had said something about further royalties, but Georgette wasn't sure that anyone would read her book. It seemed that the man was *too* nice. He hadn't made her feel like the dowdy old maid at all, and he'd complimented her book so nicely. She appreciated gentlemen who had the foresight to treat her as a lovely woman even when she knew otherwise.

What she needed most, Georgette thought, was a davenport or Chesterfield and armchairs. That would take her two to three books. If she had been able to write a story about her neighbors and then write them fantastical ends, could she write a story without using them at all? Perhaps she could take them as they had been at the end of the book—different from how she knew them now—and add another character like Mr. Aaron had suggested. Perhaps…Mr. Aaron himself? Mischief had her grinning and she debated only long enough to decide playing with the idea couldn't hurt.

Georgette and Eunice ate their simple dinner that evening, and then Georgette turned her attention to the tea and the cake. Each bite was a vacation for her taste buds. Mrs. Hannigan was a woman who was crotchety as an old man in chronic pain, but the woman could bake a cake. Georgette lifted her list of things they could use for the house. She felt a rush of her heart going mad and her blood racing through her body and something of a sickness to her stomach that she would like to blame on the cake, but was certainly caused by her thoughts.

"Miss Georgie?" Eunice frowned at the cake. As though she couldn't have made a cake for Miss Georgie and it be as good as anything that Mrs. Hannigan would make and cost half as much as well.

"Eunice?" Georgette replied. "Did you eat some cake? I hope you did."

"You ate enough for both of us, Miss Georgie, and you'll be sick for it."

"Perhaps so, dear Eunice, but I have no regrets about the cake."

"Remember that when you're sicking up later. I'm going to my bedroom unless you need anything else?"

Georgette shook her head and Eunice cleared away the remnants of the cake. The evening had changed to full night while Georgette dreamed over what she had done and whether she were mis-remembering. She had pulled out the contract from Mr. Aaron and the letter from him more than once just to verify it hadn't all been a wild dream.

This surreal haze that she was in. It was more than just impossible. It was unbelievable, and yet it was something *she had done.* She felt this sense of freedom, of near flight. She had made money on her own. She had changed her state. She...she...she had a path laid out for her and never expected anything more. Her fate, up until she'd picked up her pen, had been to be lonely and poor. Her fate had been to be the town's old maid until she finally passed away, leaving behind none who would regret or miss her.

With the state of her dividends, Georgette had expected even less than the life her parents had left. With the change in the world's finances, Georgette had expected to become poorer and poorer until instead of dying alone in her cottage, she died alone in a debtor's hovel.

Now, however, she had done something entirely different. She had put enough money in her account to correct the overdraft, but she had also stepped off the path she had been given. If she had written and sold a book, what else was possible?

CHAPTER 4

HARRIET LAWRENCE, MISERABLE WIFE

There was nothing that Georgette wanted more than to see Mrs. Harriet Lawrence (or anyone) open up her crisp new copy of *The Chronicles of Harper's Bend* several months later. As Mrs. Lawrence often did, she waited until after supper to curl up with her book. Her husband, Bertrand, was an author who wrote moralistic treatises and essays on modern behavior. He wrote in the evenings, often into the night, never realizing that she loved that he did. She had realized that he thought he was somehow punishing her by making himself unavailable during traditional family time.

She smiled as she opened the book, pausing to think of her husband's books. He had an unaccountably rabid audience. Harriet would never admit to it to her husband, but she found his books and theories ridiculous, only outpaced by the stupidity of his audience. If someone could pin her opinion on his work down—and they could not—she would describe his audience as a group of sheep who had joined the undeserved and unworthy cult of Bertrand Lawrence.

The first page of *The Chronicles of Harper's Bend* introduced the delightful Dr. Williams. How funny, Harriet thought, that the Dr. Williams in the fictional village was so like the Dr. Wilkes in her hometown. They both had ruddy cheeks and brilliant green eyes.

As Harriet read on, she choked when she saw that the baker, Mrs. Hallingson, had the same mannerisms as her village's Mrs. Hannigan. What were the chances? It was then that Harriet paused and her head tilted. Her dark eyes fixed on the page, and she tucked her hair behind her ear.

"No," Harriet whispered, as Mrs. Hallingson in the book shamed a Mrs. Evans for buying her children a cake rather than making it herself. In the background, a set of three spoiled baker's daughters whined about having to knead the bread in the voice of high-pitched rodents, and Harriet burst into laughter. She repeated, "No! Surely not!"

Harriet flipped back to the early pages and re-read how the village was set between two hills with a stream that wound down along the side of the village. Bard's Crook was situated in just that way. She nibbled her bottom lip and flipped forward. The teashop on the corner of High Street and Lavender Lane, Bard's Crook had a teashop on the corner of High Street and Hibiscus Street.

She knew then for certain, of course. What the author had done didn't truly strike Harriet until she met Lawrence Bennet in the book. He was, of course, her own husband Bertrand Lawrence. Arrogant, snide, with a tendency to make women second guess everything they knew. The poor idiot, Antoinette Moore in the book (who was of course Georgette Marsh) second guessed what she knew even after she realized that there was no way she was incorrect. Harriet winced remembering that moment for Miss Marsh. Miss Marsh hadn't spoken again at the tea or the subsequent evening of cards.

Whoever this author was—they did not appreciate Bertrand. As she was alone and in the safety of her own mind, Mrs. Harriet Lawrence silently saluted the author. It was then that she pictured explaining to Bertrand the nature of the book. Her gaze widened in horror with her mind jumping ahead to how he would react. In the book, her husband attempted to romance Eliza Evans and run away with her. At the last minute, Eliza stole away with her two daughters, escaping into the night and fleeing both Bertrand and her own husband.

Harriet winced. Eliza *should* leave her husband. Harriet winced again, knowing that the remedy she prescribed for the quiet little woman was one that she could reasonably prescribe for herself. Eliza, however, had somewhere to go. Harriet, on the other hand, was not so lucky.

No. If Harriet told her husband what she discovered, he wouldn't believe her. His voice would chill at first, and he would mock her for telling him that the fiction book portrayed their home and their lives. It would take someone else. A man, in fact, to convince Bertrand Lawrence of what had occurred.

Harriet shivered as she realized what he would think if he realized she'd read the book and hadn't told him. It would only matter once he believed. Did she tell him? Did she not? She bit her lip and then as she heard him shut his office door and head up the stairs, she quickly turned out the light, shoving the book under the mattress, and pretended to sleep.

He opened the door a moment later. The creak of it should have been fixed long ago, but Bertrand didn't help about the house. He harrumphed and turned on the light. If she had been asleep, it would have woken her. She carefully remained still and breathed evenly as he stomped across the room, opening the wardrobe. She heard his clothes land in a pile on the chair and the sound of him getting into his pajamas. When he stood as he pulled them up, he caught his big toe in the leg—as he often did—and tripped.

If she felt free to express her opinion, she would suggest shorter pajamas pants for him or encourage him to remember that he tripped over them every third day. Instead, she kept still. As usual, he cursed aloud and then thundered across the floor, plopping onto the bed.

She should be able to get away with pretending to sleep through him. She'd done it often enough. Though sometimes the best choice was to wake and offer to get him a glass of warm milk or offer to heat him a water bottle for his feet. Alternatively, however, if he were warm, he would snap at her if she offered, perhaps even engage in a diatribe of her general stupidity.

Harriet kept her eyes closed as he slapped the blankets back, half uncovering her before he pulled them over his body and then harrumphed loudly. The fool had left the light on, and she was sure he didn't want to get up and turn it off. He groused and shuffled about, sighing deeply.

Harriet would have rolled her eyes, but she was pretending to be asleep. With a slow yawn, she opened her eyes, pretending to wake and smiled a lie of a greeting at him.

"Hello, darling," she said in a low, sweet voice. "I hope your evening was excellent."

He scowled at her as she sat up and pushed back her covers.

"I'll get the light, shall I? Would you like anything?"

It was the right move. He scowled fiercely at her and harrumphed again before flopping onto his side and taking her pillow. "Just the light."

She rose and crossed to the light switch, keeping a pleasant smile on her face until the light was out. The moment she was concealed by darkness she shot a furious look to the form of her husband and took one of the cushions from the window seat before returning to the bed. She was careful to slide softly into bed and placed the cushion under her head.

She did not, however, sleep. She considered how to get the book out of her house before she was caught with it. She waited until Bertrand was snoring deeply and then slipped from the bed, into her robe, and read through the night. In the morning, she buried the book in a basket under her mending, dressed before Bertrand woke, and then slipped out the door—basket in hand. She'd have breakfast with her friends, do some mending, and return without the book.

Harriet needed to speak immediately with her friends, Virginia Baker or Theodora Wilkes. Either could be trusted with the news in the book and keeping Harriet out of it. She wanted the news of the book to come out. Her husband deserved the censure in it, and hopefully she could persuade one of the ladies to pass it along to a man with a large mouth. Perhaps Mr. Thornton or Peter Hadley.

～

THE EARLY READERS

Mr. Peter Hadley was a man who adored herbs. They were simple things on the surface, with untold depths. There was borago officinalis: if taken after a long night of drinking, it would help the indulger recover. His favorite, however, was taraxacum officinale, which made a rather delightful wine. Mr. Hadley had his own batches running and gifted them often.

In between foraging for herbs, Mr. Hadley loved to read. So much so that he had a subscription and ordered books by their covers or titles alone. He was rather good friends with several readers in other towns, and they exchanged books regularly. At the moment that he was gathering young dandelion leaves, a package was arriving with *Jamaica Inn* by Daphne du Maurier, *The Chronicles of Harper's Bend* by Joseph Jones, and *Death in the Stocks* by Georgette Heyer.

One village away, Stevenson Books received a box of recent releases from Aaron & Luther publishing. The proprietor, Dennis Stevenson flipped through the pages of *The Chronicles of Harper's Bend*, noted the description of the village, and set aside a copy to read himself. He was quite familiar with Bard's Crook and recognized the similarities immediately. As Stevenson hadn't heard of Joseph Jones, he wondered if it wasn't the pseudonym of someone he knew tangentially.

In the library, Miss Juliette Hallowton opened her own box of recent acquisitions. She'd read the description of *The Chronicles of Harper's Bend* the week before and ordered it along with several other books. Miss Hallowton needed to catalogue all of the books, but she thought she might start with this little book by Joseph Jones. It did sound delightful, and the early reviews were quite fervent.

CHAPTER 5

THEODORA WILKES, DOCTOR'S WIFE

"I'll deliver it, darling," the doctor's wife, Theodora Wilkes, told her oldest friend, Harriet Lawrence. Theodora eyed her friend carefully. Should she offer Harriet a home again? How did you divorce a man if he wasn't having an affair and wasn't beating you? Was it enough that he was cold, cruel, condescending, and an out and out rotter? Oh, if only, Theodora thought, if only you could take evidence of being a bastard to the courts and free yourself from your childhood idiocy.

Next to them, Virginia Baker's mouth twisted. She was a widow herself, but she'd just as soon have Francis back. Harriet might ache for freedom from her husband, but perhaps she'd think otherwise if she knew how hard it was to get by when you were used to having your bills paid. Francis hadn't been a good lover or kind or particularly nice to be around. Francis had, however, earned quite a lot of money, and she very much wanted to replace her wardrobe and perhaps even have a trip to Paris.

"Darling," Virginia said, sipping her tea and glancing around the parlor. She didn't mend clothes, of course, so she'd been flipping through the book. "Am I in the book?"

Harriet's lips pressed together, gaze darting to the side as she winced. "You won't like it."

"Won't I?" Virginia grinned charmingly. "Why wouldn't I?"

"I'm sure you remember your—ah…friendship from last winter?"

Virginia paused, her eyes narrowing on Harriet. No one had known about that except for Theodora and Harriet. Virginia had been trying to determine if his income was what he pretended it to be. It hadn't been, and there had been quite a ruckus between the two of them at their parting. He'd fled back to Leeds, and she'd bemoaned liars to her friends.

"What about that liar?" Virginia snapped, recalling the rage of the previous year when she'd realized her lover was poorer than herself.

"Your—ah…relationship is…illustrated in the book," Harriet said carefully.

Relationship was hardly the term, Theodora thought. Her marriage to the doctor was a relationship. Even, Harriet's sham of a marriage was more of a relationship. What Virginia had with that traveling boarder had been a hunt on both sides—each of them looking for a rich spouse.

Theodora shifted and Harriet glanced her way. There was a weighted glance of understanding between the married friends and Virginia glanced between them. They had been the only ones who'd heard Virginia's vocalized fury. "But neither of you wrote the book?"

"Of course we didn't," Theodora told Virginia. "You know that we didn't."

"Then how did anyone know about that?"

"We don't know what your—ah…friend said or did."

Virginia paled. "You don't think—"

Theodora glanced at Virginia, hiding a snap of anger at the woman. Of *course* she thought that the man Virginia had strung along didn't feel he owed her anything, including privacy. Theodora also thought that Virginia was far less sly than she imagined herself to be. Anyone who paid attention would have realized there was a flirtation between Virginia Baker and the boarder. Anyone who knew Virginia very well knew that she'd been far more interested in the income that had led to a such a fine quality auto and a traveling life of leisure.

"We can't let it get out!" Virginia hissed. "I'm sorry Harriet. Theodora, you can't give that book to anyone. This secret must remain between us. If...if...Mr. Hadley finds out. I've just gotten past his shyness."

Harriet started and begged her friend Theodora to step in. Bertrand didn't get violent often, but...Harriet cast a pleading gaze to the doctor's wife who tried to silently assure her friend. If Theodora had to choose between her friend the widow and her friend the harassed wife, Theodora would choose Harriet every single time.

"There is no way to prevent this from getting out," Harriet told Virginia gently—inside she was bemoaning her choice to say anything in front of Virginia. It wasn't like Harriet hadn't known the woman was selfish! It wasn't like the whole of Bard's Crook didn't know what the widow was like. The only person she was fooling was herself and possibly that rich herbalist, Mr. Hadley.

"We can *try*," Virginia snapped.

"Miss Marsh, Mr. Hadley, Mr. Smith, myself, my husband, the librarian, the vicar, they're all great readers. All of us have book subscriptions. All of us purchase books frequently and share amongst ourselves," Theodora said gently. "One of them will read it, and it'll be out."

"No!" Virginia cried. "No, no, no! You don't understand, I need to marry again. I must get Mr. Hadley to fall in love with me."

Theodora glanced at Harriet, who was still silently pleading, and then Harriet turned back to Virginia, hiding a scowl.

"Then," Theodora snapped, "I suppose you'll need to get him in your web by then." She knew her husband would frown at her for being churlish, but he was kind all of the time. It was the caregiver in him.

"What is that supposed to mean?" Virginia demanded.

"Virginia you are beautiful, eloquent," Theodora stumbled a little for further attributes and then covered for herself by reaching out to take hold of the woman's hand. With her free hand, Theodora reached out to Harriet. "There is much for men to adore about you, and you'll find the right one."

"My debts have come due now!" Virginia hissed, blinking her eyes rapidly to pretend at a rush of tears. "I'm going to be out of date and dumpy as Georgette Marsh if I'm not careful to find someone soon."

Theodora winced and rose, pulling Harriet up as well. "Virginia dear, have a little faith that fate will be kind to you and you'll find another man who will adore you as much as Francis did."

Virginia huffed at that thought, casting a bemoaning look at her friends. "Promise me you won't say anything."

Harriet was the one who replied and Theodora was grateful for it, because it wasn't a promise that she would be making.

"I won't say a word," Harriet swore. She smiled softly and told herself that no one had to know that she'd read the book.

Theodora and Harriet left Virginia's home a moment later, both of them reflecting upon their friend. Virginia Baker was rather a good friend when she wanted to be, but she was inclined towards focusing on her own problems. For Virginia, having enough money for the season's new clothes was far more important than how your husband treated you. It wasn't an attitude that either Theodora or Harriet understood, but then again, Virginia wasn't as soft as the other two women, and there was no question who ruled the house where Virginia lived.

For Harriet—she'd rather be married to a poor but kind man. For Theodora who was married to a man who adored her, she knew the worth of her man. It was Eliza and Harriet, her two friends with cruel husbands, that kept Theodora ever grateful for her sweet doctor. Sometimes, Theodora thought, you had to see how others suffered to recognize that even with weakened lungs from her last bought of the influenza, she had too many blessings to count.

Theodora walked Harriet and her mending home, hearing the snap of Bertrand's voice as he demanded where his wife had flitted off to, while she walked on. She had been increasing her strength day by day after her illness and should be able to make it to visit Mr. Thornton. First, however, she sat down on a bench on the green and opened *The Chronicles of Harper's Bend.* Perhaps Harriet was jumping to assumptions.

A few hours later when Theodora closed the book, she realized that Harriet was absolutely correct. She stood and made her way to the Thornton house, knowing she'd find the man of the house in the garden. She laughed as she angled down his lane, thinking of the way Joseph Jones illustrated the way Mr. Thornton changed his will over and over again, let alone the life the author had given to his eyebrows.

"Hullo, hullo, Mr. Thornton."

"Hello, my dear." Mr. Thornton waggled those prodigious eyebrows and said, "Bit of a walk for you all the way over here. Would you like a ride home?"

"Oh no, oh Mr. Thornton!" She put on her most distressed voice. "Oh! I have just been reading the most…ah—*concerning* book. I do wonder if you'd lend me your expert opinion."

Mr. Thornton lifted his brows up and down several times and then cleared his throat. "Of course, my dear. Of course. No need to put a frown on that pretty face. Tell me all about it."

Mrs. Wilkes smiled at him, hiding her reaction to his rescuing words and told herself that she'd both set him up for such a reaction, and she had known who she was dealing with before she approached his garden gate.

She widened her eyes big and fluttered her lashes, pretending to be unable to find the words before she finally poured the whole tale of *The Chronicles of Harper's Bend* on his ear.

"Oh my dear," he said, clearing his throat and moving those brows of his about. "I can't imagine you are correct. Probably just a few odd coincidences. Nothing to concern your pretty little head over. Now, tell me about the children."

Theodora took his hand as she gushed, "You are too good to me Mr. Thornton, and I *do so* appreciate it. I wonder, however, if you might read the book for me? Just to assure me? I would feel ever so much better."

Mr. Thornton agreed before she'd even finished asking, and she pressed the book into his hand and then told him about how her boys, Martin and Denford, had put a frog in Nanny's knitting and stolen the pie tarts. Cook had been ever so angry until she realized that the boys had given them to the Evans girls. Those girls did need something to brighten their days. Martin and Denford didn't understand being worn down by an angry Papa. Their father was, of course, doting.

Mr. Thornton chuckled over the nervousness of women as he went into the house after finishing the work in his garden. He washed up and requested a pot of coffee to his office. He took a long sip of his coffee and laughed again. Women! He leaned back into his chair, opened the book, and sniffed. He'd read this book, assure Mrs. Wilkes, and then go over to the pub for a pint before returning home.

Perhaps on the way, he'd stop by his son Gregory's house, to see if he'd gone to work that day. The boy had a good enough job as a barrister, but he really did need to show up at the office to be able to bill his clients.

The moment Mr. Thornton discovered a 'Mrs. Morton,' the former factory worker who ran a book club and ladies' club with an iron hand, he knew that someone had written about his wife. When he read about the changing will, his jaw dropped, his gaze lit with fury and he charged to his feet.

"Something must be done!" he shouted at the maid, moving his eyebrows to emphasize the sheer level of his fury, and then stopped with his brows stuck in a surprised position. He had read what Jones had said about the way Mr. Thornton moved his eyebrows, and now it seemed that they were more aliens on his forehead than parts of his body.

The idiot girl jumped back, cowering from him, and he cursed at her and left the room. He didn't bother with his wife who would reach a level of anger he wasn't prepared to handle. Instead he rushed over to Lawrence's house. Bertrand would know what to do. He was a writer. People followed his prescribed way of life. Bunch of nonsense really, that codswallop that Bertrand wrote, but he knew things about the way of the world. The book world, in particular.

CHAPTER 6

MRS. AGNES THORNTON, FORMER FACTORY WORKER

*T*he story of *The Chronicles of Harper's Bend* flew through Bard's Crook on the wings of Pheme, goddess of rumors. It went from house to house, from friend to friend until every single copy within distance had been purchased, some had been burned, and a few neighbors who had learned too late about the book had to send all the way to London for a copy.

Harriet Lawrence was pretending obliviousness while her husband's gaze settled on her far too often. Eliza Evans, whose fictional self had left her husband in the nighttime, had been sent to her sister-in-law at Lyme for a few weeks by the sea. Carola Matthews who was not portrayed in the book at all, burned three copies, and refused to consider whether this mad 'Joseph Jones' had based the idiocy on Bard's Crook at all.

Mr. Evans attacked Mr. Lawrence in the local pub when someone made a joke about Eliza leaving her husband for Lawrence and then leaving him high and dry as well. It was a great joke until three people were left with black eyes, one person was left with a broken nose, and too many pint glasses were broken. The fight ended with a roar and everyone who had been portrayed in the book was booted from the establishment.

Mr. Thornton had known about the book for days when Mrs. Thornton read it. She was left in a speechless rage that turned into a cold, seething fury. Mr. Thornton had been quite upset, but he didn't understand the horror of having one's past paraded out for all to digest. A worker. A factory worker! She didn't even admit to herself that it had been her past. Changing it slightly and putting it in a book? For anyone to read and know? Something must be done.

"Something must be done," she told her husband, in the tone that had once given him nightmares.

"Ah," Mr. Thornton said, "my dear..."

"*Something* must be done," Mrs. Thornton said again, each word a precise exclamation that had Mr. Thornton twitching.

"Of course," he said, frantically wondering what *could* be done. "I'll talk to my lawyer immediately."

"We will find out who wrote this," Mrs. Thornton said evenly. "Invite everyone. Gather them up. They won't be able to hide. They'll see. They'll learn."

Mr. Thornton nodded to his wife, but in his mind, he was wondering exactly how he could protect her from the crimes she was dreaming up.

GEORGETTE MARSH, SECRET AUTHOR

"Miss Georgie?"

Eunice stood in the doorway of Georgette Marsh's bedroom where she was surprised she was working on her new book. It was just—she *did* so want new clothes. She'd purchased used shoes when she'd gotten her old ones re-soled, and the new ones were delightfully comfortable. They fit ever so much better than the hand-me-downs she'd been wearing. After Georgette corrected her bank account, and re-filled her pin money, further fripperies had to wait. Clothes, however, let alone furniture for the parlor—those were on her dream list. Possibly painting her little cottage—how nice would that be?

Georgette looked up from her newest book and laughed at Eunice, mocking those 'big' dreams driving the writing. Georgette was secretly thrilled with her newest book and with writing. She could hardly believe that she'd written this one from her *own* imagination, but she had! Well, mostly she had. This one was still set in Bard's Crook a la Harper's Bend, but it focused on the fate of an entirely fictional family. Well, mostly fictional. She'd taken a dash of her own mother and father to create the couple who had come to live in Harper's Bend with their adult son, Chester Alvin.

The character was, she supposed, a bit of a fictional version of her Mr. Charles Aaron. It wasn't *really* him. Rather it was based off of him as she'd met him that single afternoon. She'd taken him right out of his office and his…did gentlemen such as him go to clubs still? Did he ride in a cab or drive an auto? Perhaps he took a bus to work?

Regardless of what he did in his real life, the fictional version of him had been taken away from everything he'd known and thrown to the lions in her village. She *was* having the most fun torturing him and them. Would he see himself in the book? If he realized what she'd done, would he be amused? Perhaps horrified? Outraged like her neighbors?

The real Mr. Aaron, she told herself, she did not know at all. This person in her book wasn't him. He'd never know what she'd done. She never really expected her first book to make its way to her village. Maybe she'd have been more clever in disguising things if she'd ever thought…ever imagined…but who could?

Georgie gasped and turned, "Oh Eunice! I didn't—" Georgette rubbed her brow and smiled at the maid. "I suppose I was somewhere else."

"You're wanted somewhere else," Eunice said dryly. She crossed to Georgette's table, straightening the pile of papers and picking up the balled-up paper that was decorating the bedroom floor.

Georgette frowned and then heard Eunice laugh darkly. With a frown, Georgette asked, "Whatever is the matter? Where could I be wanted? I am working."

Eunice scoffed. She knew well enough what the 'good' folk of Bard's Crook thought of her Miss Georgie. Fools, the lot of them. Never realizing that Miss Marsh was playing the part they'd given her. Putting Miss Marsh into the role of old maid before she'd been twenty, and never once had her girl fought her way out of it. "There is a town meeting at the church. It seems the esteemed villagers of Bard's Crook would like to discuss the recent outrage."

"The outrage?" Georgette did not trust that tone in Eunice's voice.

The woman grinned wickedly and then returned to picked up the floor.

"Eunice? The outrage? Eunice, don't pick those up. My goodness, I wouldn't have thrown those papers down if I'd expected you to pick them up."

"Don't worry about the papers, Miss Georgie. Worry about this gathering."

Georgette rubbed her brow and she helped picked up the rejected portions of her book. "Whatever is happening?"

"It seems *The Chronicles of Harper's Bend* and that fiend, the author, deserves to be drawn and quartered. Our neighbors are meeting to discuss just such an event."

Georgette's gaze widened and she gasped. "No!"

"Yes."

"But...how *do they know?*"

"That remains to be seen," Eunice said, with that same pragmatism that attended the whole of Georgette Marsh's life. "You'll need to go, however, to find out what they know."

Georgette bit down on her bottom lip and then nodded. Her heart was hovering around the back of her throat, and her stomach seemed to have dropped to her waist.

"Go change," Eunice ordered.

Georgette nodded and hurried into the bath. She examined her face in the mirror and then scrubbed the ink from her fingers. No need to give them clues to who was the author. She washed her face and ran a brush through her hair. If she'd had an ounce of vanity, she'd have scowled into her mirror, but Georgette had long since made peace with her pale skin, freckles, and often too ruddy cheeks.

Georgette examined her dress. It had once been a soft grey, but over time, she'd been forced to dye it dark grey to hide the forming discoloration. Neither the light or darker grey had done anything for Georgette's coloring. If anything, the current grey made her look sickly. She'd have glanced through her armoire, but she already knew she didn't have a better option. She just ensured the dress wasn't too wrinkled, put a jumper over the top, and placed a barrette on the side of her face to keep her hair from falling forward.

"You can't turn a duck into a swan, miss," Georgette told herself without an ounce of sympathy for her vanity.

The walk to the church where the town hall meeting was taking place wasn't long, but Georgette would have wished it were quite a bit longer. Nothing was very far in Bard's Crook, which did make getting around on foot all the easier.

Georgette considered her book as she walked, a distant look on her face. Did they know that *she* had written it? What *was* she walking into? Who had read the book? It had only been a few weeks since it had been published. Did they hate her for what she'd done? They must. Of course they did, if they were calling her book an outrage.

Her mind flicked over the story and she realized that perhaps she could have been kinder. She would have been—perhaps—maybe. How could she have expected the portraits she'd written over her neighbors to ever reach them?

She scolded herself as she strode on. You wrote that book, Georgie! You wrote it and you sold it and you *knew* it would be turned into something to be sold to the world at large. Someone was going to read it. But—so many books were published that never made their way to Bard's Crook. Why should hers arrive here?

She had received a praise-filled letter from Mr. Aaron saying that sales were going well. He'd recommended in that letter that she should subscribe to the periodicals that wrote reviews, and she'd done so, but she hadn't dared to read the reviews yet.

That letter could have meant anything. It didn't have to mean that her story had reached the hands of those who she lived nearby. Oh, she could have been much kinder. She nibbled her bottom lip as she considered the endings she'd given some of her neighbors. It was just that—well, if she must be honest with herself, she didn't like very many of them very much, and it appeared in her work.

It was that very hesitant, very guilty, very inexplicably blank expression that had Virginia Baker grabbing hold of Theodora Wilkes and holding her back from joining Miss Marsh on the walk to the Thornton home.

"Darling," Mrs. Wilkes, the doctor's wife, said, "it's just Miss Marsh. She's harmless."

"I don't call that inane look on her face harmless. It makes my skin fair crawl. Why is she coming to this? Do you think she's even read *The Chronicles of Harper's Bend?*"

"Virginia," Mrs. Wilkes said, "I'm surprised at you. I quite like Miss Marsh. Outside of that, she's *in* the book, how could we leave her out of this meeting?"

"You like everyone," Mrs. Baker said with a deep frown. "I don't know why. I am certain she hasn't even read the book. She's probably just come for the tea, weak bathwater though it'll be."

"She's come because she's been requested, as we all have," Mrs. Wilkes replied, breaking free of Mrs. Baker's grasp. "Oh Miss Marsh! How delightful to meet you." Mrs. Wilkes flinched a little, knowing her greeting was too effusive, but her own guilt had her acting far more warmly than she might have otherwise.

Virginia muttered crossly under her breath and Georgette turned to smile at the duo. Mrs. Baker the grasping widow who lived far beyond her means and Mrs. Wilkes, the beloved doctor's wife and one of the few people in Bard's Crook that Georgette appreciated. She had, of course, seen them as she approached. Standing in the shadows of an oak tree might be an excellent hiding place if it were evening. Perhaps even at dusk. But with the sun high overhead? No, it didn't work at all.

She smiled as the two women waited for her to draw even with them, then they carried on together.

"She hasn't read it!" Mrs. Baker hissed to Mrs. Wilkes when Georgette was clearly in earshot. "Do you think she even understands anything beyond a basic primer?"

"Virginia!" Mrs. Wilkes scolded, aghast. "Miss Marsh is too sweet."

Miss Marsh considered that attribute and knew that it was given to her because Mrs. Wilkes didn't know Georgette all that well. After all, how sweet could she be when she'd sent Mrs. Baker fleeing the village pursued by her creditors? Georgette had returned the woman in the second book in reduced circumstances and forced to wear last season's clothing, but no one knew that yet.

Mrs. Baker seemed to think Georgette was deaf as well as blind. She used her old trick of focusing just beyond the shoulder of the woman she despised and smiled fiercely at the devil she was sure was hovering nearby. If she believed in devils on a person's shoulder, Mrs. Virginia Baker certainly had two—one full of avarice and the other full of needless cruelty.

The idea of it had Miss Marsh giving another, brighter smile, which further endeared her to Mrs. Wilkes. She *had* been afraid that Miss Marsh might have heard that last comment from Virginia. Certainly not, though, with such a sweet smile. "Hello, dear. Isn't this weather horrid?"

"It's what makes it so green and beautiful here," Miss Marsh said quite happily. She loved a good drizzle. The world smelled so fresh and new after a drizzle. Her hair became frizzier with the weather, but Miss Marsh didn't see the harm in that. Frizzy or plastered to the side of her head, she didn't have the lovely curls of the two women in front of her.

"Ah," Mrs. Baker said, not even hiding her snide sideways glance before she frowned ahead of them. "It ruins my hair!"

"You always look lovely," Miss Marsh replied. A simple truth, though she didn't really feel it was much of a compliment. Anyone who spent as much time and effort working on her face and hair really should have something to show for her efforts. How sad would it be to work so hard and still be as homely as Miss Marsh herself?

"Do you know what this is all about?" Mrs. Wilkes asked kindly. Someone needed to explain to the poor Miss Marsh.

In an act of sheer daring, Miss Marsh said, "I understand there's an uproar about a book? What a funny idea to get so upset over words on a page!"

"Have you read it?" Mrs. Baker's snide voice snapped.

Really! The woman should at least try to sound more pleasing. She had her eye on the rich herbalist who was too sweet to succumb to just a pretty face. At least, Miss Marsh hoped he was too sweet for such a fate. If she were more of a meddler, she'd take him aside and direct his attention to the librarian, Miss Hallowton, or any other female.

"I'm familiar with it," Miss Marsh said vaguely. An idea struck her all at once, and her gaze darted about guiltily before she reined herself in. Did she dare?

"What did you think of the book?" Mrs. Wilkes asked gently.

"I quite liked how well it was written," Miss Marsh said, tucking her hair behind her ear and keeping her gaze quite firmly focused on the ground ahead of them. She doubted either of them would be able to see the lie in her gaze, but Eunice would have known that Miss Marsh was telling a whopper the second their gazes met.

Mrs. Wilkes cleared her throat softly, giving Miss Marsh another sharp jab of guilt before the other woman asked, "Did you notice anything—ah—familiar in the story?"

"Such as?" Miss Marsh asked vaguely, keeping her gaze tucked away. If they didn't *know* it was her who'd written it, maybe she wouldn't get...strung up? What had Eunice said? Drawing and quartering?

When she'd written the book, the conclusion she'd created for Mrs. Baker had felt natural. She'd been engaged to one of the local lads, discovered he'd been chasing her for the income he'd *thought* she'd had, and left her at the altar. She'd been revealed as a vain, cruel woman in the book, but now that they were walking side-by-side,

Miss Marsh felt...mean? Something akin to mean without getting there. It wasn't as though Mrs. Baker were a kind woman who had been maligned.

"It's about us, you ninny! You're even in it."

Miss Marsh's heart seized as she smiled vaguely at the other woman. "That can't be right. There wasn't a Mrs. Baker in the story."

"You fool!" Mrs. Baker snapped. "I was Verinda Cooke."

Miss Marsh wasn't sure how she kept her face blank when she said, "Oh no, Mrs. Baker that can't be right. Mrs. Cooke was covetous and quite—well—loose."

Mrs. Wilkes cleared her throat and took Miss Marsh's arm. "Yes. Well. Perhaps not."

Miss Marsh smiled at the devil just beyond Mrs. Baker's shoulder, knowing that her own spiteful devil was out and out gleeful.

CHAPTER 7

GEORGETTE MARSH, SECRET AUTHOR

"You all know why we've come." Mr. Thornton stood, turning on his neighbors. They were using the large room beyond the sanctuary, but the chairs were all still filled, with gentlemen leaning against the wall at the back of the room as well.

Mrs. Thornton grumbled under her breath and shot her neighbors a threatening glance every time they *dared* to meet her gaze. They had *better* not look at her with that judging gaze.

The room was quite crowded with those who had been mentioned in the book in some way or the other. Georgette saw Dr. Wilkes at the same moment as his wife who crossed immediately to him. They had little to complain of as far as their treatment in the book had gone.

Did Georgette feel repentant? She considered the state of her restored bank account, the agony of realizing she couldn't continue to survive, and realized that as upset as her neighbors were—she was more grateful she'd discovered a way to change her fate.

Perhaps she had been very unkind. Perhaps she should have

written from her imagination, but she hadn't been able to. She *had* tried. She'd stared at blank pages for days upon days before she decided to catalogue a funny little incident between Mr. Thornton and his sons. Things just flew away from her after that moment.

Miss Marsh had been much kinder to several who hadn't bothered to come, while those who had more room for complaint were scowling about as though they could startle their neighbors into confessing who had written it. Miss Marsh took a solitary chair in the corner, avoided every gaze, and nibbled her bottom lip. She silently ordered herself to give no reaction and continue to be the fool they expected her to be.

It was quite uncomfortable, but not as uncomfortable as the taste of the tea on her tongue. Were they using just twigs and branches to flavor this? Who had donated it? It might actually be worse than what she had been drinking before her book had sold. Another thing, she thought, to add to her list of reasons to keep on writing. She could afford tea that was more than herbs dried from her own garden. She sipped her tea with a vague smile, dreaming of the new oolong that Eunice had just brought home. It was divine.

"I haven't read the book," Mr. Hadley, the herbalist said carefully, clearing his throat and pushing back his glasses, "yet, I can't see why everyone is quite so upset. Perhaps we should take a moment to reflect."

Mr. Thornton almost growled as his eyebrows thundered terrifyingly. "Read it you demmed fool! Then come here with those inanities."

"He doesn't have much to complain of. The author was nice to him!" Mrs. Thornton snapped. "Perhaps *he* wrote it. Prosing on about lavender and roses and roots and other such nonsense and then secretly writing this...this...travesty!"

"Perhaps we should look at those who are treated well in the book instead of just ignored! Dr. Wilkes, what about you? Whoever wrote this book is fair in love with you." Mr. Lawrence sniffed. "Unlike me. Treating my wife like an animal. Mocking my work and my audience." The flush on his ears showed he knew exactly how he treated his wife.

Mr. Lawrence continued on, "Trying to steal another man's wife. And! And! My books! As though my books aren't respected treatises on behavior and thought!"

Thornton grumbled and then shouted, "No one cares about your demmed books. Almost as foolish as this evil book! I demand to know who the author is! I demand the name! I demand justice!"

"How dare you compare my treatises to those…those Chronicles of Idiocy?" Mr. Lawrence shouted back.

"Enough!" Dr. Wilkes snapped. He didn't shout, but the command in his voice had the other men falling silent. "Turning on each other is not going to help your cause."

"Don't you care?" Mr. Thornton demanded.

"Of course he doesn't care," Mrs. Baker inserted. "Why should he? This Jones fellow wasn't unkind to him. Unlike you. Unlike me."

Mrs. Baker knew all too well that Mr. Lawrence was, in fact, quite cruel to poor Harriet, who hadn't even come to this meeting, but the chance of Eliza Evans leaving her husband, let alone for another man was laughable. That portion of the book was pure fiction, since the woman would suffer in silence, doing her duty until she faded into the wind.

"My wife," Mr. Evans growled behind Miss Marsh. "Mine."

Miss Marsh glanced around the room, nibbling her bottom lip and avoiding every gaze. Had any author ever been part of *such* a scene? She had thought that selling her book and making actual money from it would be the most surreal she had ever felt, but she couldn't have imagined this moment.

"That's right," Thornton said, "he wasn't cruel to you, doctor. Why not? *Did* you write it?"

"Of course I didn't," Dr. Wilkes replied evenly, calm in the face of the other's rage. "I barely have time to spend with my wife and children when I'm not working. I assure you I don't have time for any such nonsense."

Miss Marsh had flinched when they turned on Dr. Wilkes. She had been kind to him in the book and to Mrs. Wilkes as well as to a few others. Miss Marsh had been kind to Patricia Nunn and her neighbor Mr. Jilly who both had received a happier ending —together.

Miss Marsh had been quite kind to Miss Hallowton who had received an inheritance from a distant relative, taken her savings account, and fled to distant lands to see the places she'd read and taught others about after years of being a librarian. She'd been quite kind to the widower Mr. Smith as well, but it didn't seem to matter given his expression.

Of course, Miss Marsh only remembered then that he was Mrs. Evans's brother. Mr. Smith's scowl was deep and abiding, but he didn't say a word about the book. Instead his glower moved from Mr. Lawrence to Mr. Evans. She hadn't written poor Eliza falling in love with Mr. Lawrence because Georgette thought they'd be a good match, she'd done it so that Eliza would see that there were many ways to be cruel.

Georgette wanted Eliza to leave her husband *and* avoid a repeat of the same fate with another man. For the most part, Georgette hadn't decided on story endings for the people in her book based *entirely* off of kindness or cruelty. She'd simply written about her village and then written what seemed to be the natural end to their choices.

"What I'd like to know," Mr. Evans said coolly, cutting through the shouting, "is why this author linked you to *my* wife. Explain that, Lawrence!"

Mr. Lawrence jerked back as though he'd been assaulted. "What the devil? Who knows why the fool did that? How should I know? Why would I want to be saddled with your wife when I've my own noose about my neck with Harriet?"

Theodora Wilkes gasped and Dr. Wilkes reached out to take his wife's hand, his frown turning to Lawrence. "You've a good woman in Harriet."

Mr. Lawrence sniffed and muttered, "Course I do." It wasn't heart-felt and no one felt it was true.

Miss Marsh pressed her lips together, fixing her gaze on the floor as Evans snarled, "Baker *is* a loose grasping woman."

"You devil," Virginia Baker cried, "take it back." Her eyes welled with pretty tears, but Mr. Evans carried on.

"Wilkes is a good doctor, Nunn is half in love with Jilly. Those are facts."

"But I haven't inherited anything," Miss Hallowton said gently. "Nor do I wish to take off for parts unknown. *Some* of this is fiction, Mr. Evans. I believe your wife is and always has been an honorable woman."

Mr. Evans shot the librarian a quelling look that promised more than his wife could feel the weight of his fists. "The bloke might have changed folks' names, but—*why* my wife?"

The room had fallen utterly silent when Mr. Smith rose and took Evans's arm. "That's enough, old man. You know Eliza would never leave you. Remember your wedding day. She looked at you with stars in her eyes. You've never given her a reason to feel differently, have you?"

Mr. Smith didn't have that same jolly look in his gaze that he usually did. If anything, his fingers dug a little harder into Mr. Evans's arm. The man turned on his brother-in-law, snarled something, and stormed from the room. "Stay away from my wife, Lawrence!"

Mr. Smith watched his abusive brother-in-law leave with a dawning realization of truth, Miss Marsh thought.

"You should stay away from my sister, Lawrence," Mr. Smith said, far more gently. The steel in his tone made it clear that it was an order despite the gentleness.

Mr. Lawrence cleared his throat and then glanced around. "That nonsense was at the point where everything was fiction. Quite fond of my own wife," he lied, shifting uncomfortably. "Excellent woman. Blessed man."

Mr. Thornton cleared his throat and muttered, "Something must be done."

"I tell you what we'll do," Mr. Lawrence said. "We'll visit this fool's publisher and we'll demand this book be pulled. Infamous lies and defamation. We'll sue and ruin him if he doesn't pull the book immediately."

Miss Marsh watched them carefully without ever lifting her lids and letting them see her razor attention. She might have felt worse about the argument between Evans and Lawrence, but they were both *quite* cruel to their wives and their children, and they deserved to have their little despotic kingdoms fall apart.

What terrified Miss Marsh was the threats against the kind Mr. Aaron. She must warn him, and immediately. Perhaps if she let him know, he'd be able to come up with a plan to save his business. She felt certain Mr. Thornton and Mr. Lawrence would do their best to ruin everything. Including, she slowly realized, her future and the chance of a new dress. Georgette hated that her heart was breaking more of the idea of a new dress than Mrs. Evans, but she never pretended to be a saint.

CHAPTER 8

CHARLES AARON, PUBLISHER

"Ah—" Schmitty glanced over his shoulder and then stepped into the office, shutting the door behind him. "Ah, Mr. Aaron?"

Charles looked up from the letter he'd received from the high-maintenance Thomas Spencer and scowled. "I didn't want to be bothered, Mr. Schmitt."

The poor man blushed at the snap in Charles's voice and cleared his throat. "There seems to be two gentlemen here regarding *The Chronicles of Harper's Bend.* They are…ah…outraged."

Charles leaned back, crossing his fingers over his chest. He hadn't had the chance to visit Miss Marsh in Bard's Crook yet, and a sudden chance to see exactly how good of a portrait had been drawn lured him out of his terrible mood.

Charles shot his secretary a delighted glance. "Indeed?"

"Yes, sir."

"Have you read that book?"

"Yes, sir."

"How accurate was our—" He cleared his throat and said with special inflection, "author."

"Ah." Mr. Schmitt grinned and lowered his voice. "Sir, she's a genius."

Charles also grinned. "Who have we got?"

"It is, I believe, Mr. Morton and Mr. Bennett, who have introduced themselves as Mr. Giles Thornton and Mr. Bertrand Lawrence."

Charles laughed in sheer delight. He wasn't sure if she'd selected easy names out of spite or out of laziness, but he liked that it was so overt. "Send them in. Keep your game face on. If they're ready to arm themselves, perhaps listen for cries of agony and send for the local bobby."

Schmitty was still grinning. "Would you like me to interrupt for an appointment?"

Charles shook his head. Cracking his knuckles and then shaking out his arms, he continued to smile as he said, "We're professionals here. We can handle a couple of small-town bumpkins."

The door opened and Mr. Thornton walked in first. Charles knew him immediately because of the eyebrows. He immediately imagined this man changing his will over and over again to haul his sons into line. Charles desperately wanted to know who the beneficiary of the current will was and if the solicitor charged extra for having to keep track of the old wills.

"Hello gentlemen," he greeted, standing. "To what do I owe the pleasure of this visit?" Mr. Aaron smiled vaguely and glanced between the two men.

"We're here about a crime and a travesty, and to give you the option to do the right thing," Mr. Thornton thundered.

"Indeed!" Mr. Lawrence agreed fiercely, smoothing back his hair. He lifted his left brow, and Charles had to bite back a laugh. How many times had his character lifted that brow in Miss Marsh's book? Mr. Lawrence glanced around the office with a deep scowl. "You, sir, have published an infamous and criminal book!"

Mr. Aaron sat down, refusing to let them ruffle his composure. "Have I now?"

"You have indeed, sir," Lawrence said, speaking over Thornton's thundering eyebrows. "This...this...this *Chronicles of Harper's Bend*. I will have you know, sir, that it is an infamous defamation of my character."

"A defamation?" Charles laughed, allowing a bit of contempt to cross his face. He knew too well what a little contempt could do with the right arrogant person. It was the easiest way to quell someone who assumed they were better than another. "For a fictional book?"

"It's not a fiction!" Mr. Thornton asserted in a shout.

"Gentlemen," Charles said, "I'm going to have to ask you to lower your voices or leave."

"You will be facing a lawsuit, sirrah! Are you so sure you want to laugh off this travesty?" Mr. Thornton's brows moved about his face so energetically that Charles felt the need to write Miss Marsh a note about the quality of her literary portraiture.

"Well, by all means," Charles told them, "bring your lawsuit. I find that there is very little in your abstract and vague claims that gives me pause. Let me remind you, however, that you'll need to find a lawyer willing to take such a laughable case. You'll also have to prove that this supposed 'defamation' caused you harm. A challenge I think you'll be hard-pressed to accomplish."

"I—" Mr. Lawerence began to bluster and then sniffed and fell silent.

"Indeed," Charles told him. "I believe I recognized your name. Bertrand Lawrence, the writer?"

The man nodded, adjusting his coat.

"As we're both professionals, I think we both know you don't have a case. *The Chronicles of Harper's Bend* is a charming, *fictional story* that is selling quite well. It has been, in fact, outselling your latest book by quite a measure."

Mr. Lawrence's face flushed brilliantly, but he cleared his throat and waited.

"I'm sure your publisher," Charles continued, "could not be persuaded to pull your successful book from market. You can be assured that I—despite your fervent feelings on the matter—will not be pulling an even more successful book from market simply because of vague similarities between your life and this piece of fiction."

"Are you meaning to tell me that you don't intend to comply with our wishes?" Mr. Thornton demanded. "Do you know who I am?"

"From the looks of it," Charles said calmly, allowing the attempt to filter into his voice and expression, "You are a moderately wealthy man from a small town. You are one of many such men, and I'm sure you're very important and heeded in whatever town you call home. However, I, my good man, am a business man from London and will not be bullied into losing the income for myself and my author on an excellent little book because your pride allows you to see yourself in this book."

"My pride! Well, I never!"

"By all means," Charles said generously, waving his hand, "speak to your lawyer and see what advice he has to give. As for me, I'll wait to hear from him and carry on about my business." He gestured to the door. "If you please?"

Mr. Thornton slammed to his feet, slapping his hat against his leg. "This is idiocy. You'll be hearing from me, sir!"

Charles felt a little guilt for the epic lie about the book being entirely fictional, however, he continued, "By all means, Mr. Thornton, contact your lawyer, attempt to bring this matter to the courts. You can be assured that you will have to take it that far, but I think you will discover that you have little chance of success."

Mr. Thornton didn't wait for Mr. Lawrence when he slammed out of Charles Aaron's office. Lawrence, however, paused.

"We'll take the actual name of Joseph Jones," Mr. Lawrence said, smiling a very snake-like smile. "We can handle this directly."

"I'm surprised you think I would give you that information. Mr. Jones will remain anonymous as he wishes."

"Surely the name cannot hurt?"

"Do I look like a newborn lamb making friends with the wolf, Lawrence? Out with you."

GEORGETTE MARSH, SECRET AUTHOR

Georgette missed the early train to London. She had gotten up early and found poor Eunice sicking up in the kitchen.

"Oh no!" Georgette wrapped an arm around Eunice. She'd already pulled her hair back, so Georgie rubbed Eunice's back until she calmed down, tucked her into bed with toast and tea, and then hurried out of the house.

In fact, Georgie almost missed the second train. She had to run for it and leap onto the train. She felt a bit like a woman in the pictures when she made it. She grinned widely, an action that was so rare from her, her friend might not have recognized her. Especially since the run to the train had her cheeks flushing brilliantly. She pressed her hand against her chest and opened the door to the train, making her way to a seat. The carriage was nearly full from other villages, but Georgie made her way to an empty seat on the aisle. The older gentleman by the window greeted her with a nod as she sat.

She was back to having her heart in her throat and her stomach around her waist. What if the gentlemen had gotten ahead of her? When Mr. Aaron pulled the book, would he expect her to pay back the advance? How would she be able to tell him that there was no way she could do that? What would Eunice do when Georgette had to sell the cottage and move to London for a factory job?

Georgette nibbled her bottom lip, clenching and unclenching her fists until she realized both her mouth and her forearms ached. She tried to calm down and watch through the windows as the country-side turned into the city, but instead, she found herself staring at the woman across the aisle from her.

A copy of *The Chronicles of Harper's Bend* was opened in front of her face. Georgette stared, open-mouthed. There it was! Her book! It was in the wild like some sort of rare bird. Her eyes actually welled with tears, and she found the old man sitting next to her handing her a folded handkerchief.

"Oh, I...thank you." Georgette had lost her air, so her gratitude came out like a weak whisper.

"Think nothing of it, my dear," the man said, patting her arm. "Sometimes things are just difficult."

Georgette nodded, pressing the handkerchief to her eyes. Her book, her freedom. She sniffed, watching the woman read *Chronicles*. She had finished writing the second book. Before the meeting with her neighbors about the first book, she had thought she might be able to sell the next book and even considered getting a new hat and coat. Oh, how she wanted a new hat and a coat! And a new dress. She had even made herself a list of things she'd like to replace in her wardrobe. She'd read articles about the necessary pieces of clothing. She could buy a simple skirt and several blouses with a jumper or two. With another dress for church, she'd feel like a whole new woman.

Georgette had quite adjusted to having better tea. She wasn't ready to go back. She was accustomed to sleeping through the night without worrying about how they'd survive the winter. She had become well and truly used to cream in her tea. She'd even thought of getting rid of the hen. She took a deep breath in and watched the reader laugh. She *laughed,* flipping back the pages on *Chronicles*.

By Jove! Was that woman reading the scene again? Was Georgette's book good enough that someone wanted to re-experience what she'd written? Could such things be?

Georgette pressed the handkerchief to her nose and then turned to the man. "I—"

"Keep it, my dear."

She nodded and leaned back against her seat. "Thank you."

Instead of closing her eyes, Georgette *almost* closed them, and she watched the woman with the brown tweed coat, the very dark brown cloche, and the grey curls read her book. She examined every single expression on her face as she read, watching avidly when a page was turned, and when the woman pressed a finger to the corner of her eye, Georgette had to grab onto her seat to keep herself from demanding what portion of the book brought the reader to that tear.

Was there any greater compliment than a tear? Georgette found she had to dab her own away as the train rolled to a stop. She hadn't realized that provoking an emotion from someone with her writing would mean quite so much.

She got off the train in a daze and took a black cab to the office of Mr. Aaron without even seeing London pass. Nor realizing when the black cab halted in front of the building.

"Ma'am! Ma'am!"

Georgette jerked to attention and then apologized profusely. She handed the man money and reached for the door handle. As she glanced out the window, she saw Mr. Lawrence and Mr. Thornton exit the offices of Aaron & Luther.

Georgette gasped and ordered, "Drive! Drive, my good man, drive!" She threw herself onto the seat, hiding below the windows, and curling into a ball.

The driver glanced back and then sped away.

"Are you mad, woman?"

Georgette shook her head. "Please drive for a few minutes and then return to Aaron & Luther. I'll pay you, of course."

"Of course," the man muttered, adjusting his cap on his head. He didn't bother to lower his voice as he muttered disparaging comments about women.

CHAPTER 9

CHARLES AARON, PUBLISHER

*C*harles had Schmitty bring in tea and reviewed the adjusted contract that Mrs. Ursula Blythe had returned. She was wanting a better advance but the same royalty rate. Charles stretched his neck as he considered. Unlike Thomas Spencer, the brilliant Henry Moore, or even the new Miss Marsh, Mrs. Blythe wasn't a sure bet.

He scratched the back of his head and sipped from his cup. He knew *why* she wanted the larger advance. She'd just had another baby, and she needed the money. He wasn't without sympathy, and if he thought she'd make back the advance, he'd give her the larger one. However…there was no such guarantee. It was a difficult question, one that warred between his humane tendencies and his business acumen.

"Sir?"

Charles glanced up in annoyance and then sighed. It wasn't Schmitty's fault that Charles didn't want to tell Mrs. Ursula Blythe 'no' but knew from a business perspective that he should.

"Yes?" Charles barely kept the irritation from his tone, but Schmitty knew all too well that he was angry all the same.

"Miss Marsh has arrived."

Charles was surprised at the rush of pleasure at Schmitty's announcement. "Bring her in! And more tea, Schmitty. Put sandwiches or biscuits or something on the tray."

He nodded and then paused. "She looks flustered, sir."

Charles considered the men he'd seen earlier and wondered if she knew that they were so upset. She must, of course, the poor thing. How had she discovered it all? He rose when she came into the room, and he couldn't help but note that she hadn't spent her advance on new clothes, but her face was flushed. The color brought attention to her delightful freckles. She'd pulled her hair back today, and he hadn't realized before that her face was heart shaped. You didn't notice the shape of her cheeks at first because of her freckles, but it really was quite a fine set of features.

"My dear Miss Marsh," he said, clasping the hand she gave him in both of his, "how wonderful to see you!"

"I apologize for just…just appearing. It's just when I realized they were coming, I thought I must arrive before them. Only Eunice was ill, and I had to get her settled, and I missed the first train and nearly the second and—"

Charles seated her, noting the shine in her honey brown eyes and listened as she poured out her heart. She told him about how she couldn't afford to repay the advance, and that she'd finished the next book, which she was sure he wouldn't like and as she carried on, he poured her a cup of tea.

It was oddly soothing to hear her tell the story of the meeting, and of her daring to pretend not to even understand that the book referred to her neighbors. His shout of laughter stopped her, and he handed her the tea, milky and sweet.

"I—" She blinked at him. Her lashes were darker and much thicker than he'd noted. "You're not upset?"

"No, not really." He grinned at her.

"But they want to pull it from publication. They're determined to find out who wrote it and—and—well, they want to do me harm."

"They won't lay a hand on you, my dear," he told her, finding that her gentle quietness was bringing out a bit of a ferocious protector in him. "I confess that I'm enjoying this tale and wishing very much to have been a fly on the wall in that meeting hall."

Miss Marsh smiled hesitantly at him, and he instantly wanted that surprising cheeky grin he'd glimpsed before.

"I heard, however," he said, "the mention of a second book."

She blushed brilliantly. With her pale skin and freckles, it was as though someone had set her face aflame. The purity of her reaction also charmed him. A part of Charles—the part of him that was a long-term bachelor—was wondering just why this slip of a dowdy little thing was so appealing. The part of him that was charmed felt as though he'd discovered a treasure that everyone else had overlooked.

He would very much like to see her in Bard's Crook and inter-acting with those who knew her. He would bet—no, he was certain—that they treated her like an idiot.

"I am not sure you'll like my second book," she said quietly.

"Did you continue with Harper's Bend?"

She nodded, avoiding his gaze. Her fingers were frantically moving in her lap and her ankles were firmly wrapped around each other. "It's different now. It's fictional in that nothing that is actually happening is in the book. Only little things, like how Mr. Lawrence is quite rude and how Mr. Thornton changes his will so often. Mostly it is things that I think *will* happen, but I wrote them how I prefer them to occur rather than how they did. I—" She looked away from him again and said in a lowered voice, "I added a new character. A sort of fish out of water."

"That sounds delightful," Charles assured her. He wondered if she could handle a fully fictional book. He knew, however, that *The Chronicles of Harper's Bend* had shifted from portraiture to fiction, and he hadn't noticed a change.

"I—" She shook her head and sipped her tea before she repeated, "I'm not sure you'll like it."

"Did you bring it?"

She shook her head frantically. "I really don't think you'll like it."

He grinned at her and pushed the plate of sandwiches towards her. She was too thin, he thought. He feared it was the result of too much worry and not enough to eat. "Why don't you let me be the judge of that? Shall I come to see Harper's Bend in the wild, and I'll bring you a new contract for the book?"

She shook her head.

He frowned as he examined her. "Is this because you don't think I'll like it? Or because you don't want me seen in your village?"

She dared to look at him, still blushing furiously. "I am concerned you won't wish to publish it."

"Are you worried because of how your village has already reacted?"

Her blush faded as her gaze met his. "I was not very kind to some of them, I know. I don't regret it."

His head cocked, and he waited. He wanted to know the *why* of her.

"I—I would have tried almost anything else." Her voice was barely above a whisper. "I'd have tutored girls or been a companion or worked as an assistant or a secretary, but they would never hire *me* for that kind of work. If I wanted to keep my cottage, I had to do something that was entirely unassociated with them."

He could see it. Imagine it perfectly. She truly did have a quiet demeanor. If you'd seen her through that awkward gawky stage and placed her in a category in your mind—completely unfair to judge a woman by the girl she had been—then you would miss out on what she had become.

"So, you were bound by their expectations and the way they valued you?"

She nodded.

"And, therefore, you decided to use the mind they credit you with not having to note and immortalize their behavior." Charles grinned. "What about this…I shall motor down, sit in your parlor, read this book that you believe I shall hate, and decide upon the moment? If I like it, I shall bring the contract, and we can move ahead?"

She shook her head frantically.

He reached out, taking her hand. "Miss Marsh, you trusted me with your first book. You can trust me with your second."

"I—" She glanced at him and then said very softly, "I started writing it very soon after when we spoke, and I was thrilled by the purchase of the first book, and I wasn't thinking clearly about what I was doing. Then it swept me away, and I..."

"*Why* do you think I wouldn't like it?"

"I don't want to say," she said.

"Out with it," he said, not losing his patience or his kind voice. It was just the reaction she needed to confess.

"I didn't mean to put you in it. And it's not really you." Her words were a quick rush, almost as fast as sicking up. "It's just meeting you inspired the character, and then I gave him a name kind of like yours, and I'm sorry. I didn't realize. I didn't realize that people would get so upset, but they—my village—they *hate* me because of what I wrote. They hate me, and I—I—didn't mean to do it to you too."

He laughed, and she looked up with shining eyes.

"Georgette, may I call you Georgette?"

She nodded.

"Georgette, you know Mr. Lawrence's first name?"

"Bertrand," she said.

"And the way his tea is made?"

"Always black, preferably coffee. He always makes a snide comment if you only have tea and not coffee."

Charles nodded. "Of course, I can see it now. And Thornton?"

"Tea, one sugar, no cream."

"And me?"

She looked up. "You think I haven't noticed because I've never poured for you. But you take it with no sugar and heavy on the cream."

He blinked.

"I do notice little things but that doesn't mean I know *you*."

"What if I make you a promise? That I won't take any little detail you noticed about me personally. And if this fellow you wrote about has my mannerisms or perhaps the shape of my nose or something else that you immortalized as excellently as you immortalized Mr. Thornton's eyebrows, I won't be offended."

Georgette leaned back. "Mr. Aaron—"

"Please call me Charles."

She paused. "I want you to read it first. Then we'll consider it. You saved me by buying my book, and I won't make another enemy of you. You're the only person beyond Eunice and maybe Theodora and Harriet who even notice that there is anything other than dust between my ears, and really—Theodora and Harriet barely give me the credit of sawdust over nothing at all."

He laughed again. "Is anyone else aware of how funny you are?"

She grinned and the mask she was wearing fell away entirely. Her eyes were bright and lively as her gaze met his. He felt as though, for a moment, he was the only person who was truly seeing her. "I saw someone reading my book. She laughed, re-read scenes, and cried. This perfect stranger who somehow made all that effort worthwhile. Though," she grinned wickedly, "I would have done it for the money."

Charles snorted on his laughter and then choked. There it was! That cheek, self-deprecating grin surprised him wholly and left her almost another creature. He felt as though he'd seen through a changeling to the fairy creature beneath.

"I will happily take you writing a hundred books about your variation of me, Georgette, if you will keep being as clever and well-written as you have been. We have a partnership, you and I. You write these clever books, I'll take them to market, and we'll both come out the winners. You will see me tomorrow before tea, and you will trust me with your book, because we're partners."

She still had that wicked gleam. "Well, if you're going to be that confident in it, maybe you should give me that contract now."

He paused, shocked as she lifted her brow and dared him. The rational businessman told him not to do it, but the cultivator of art and partnerships such as this one nodded and rang the bell for Schmitty.

CHAPTER 10

GEORGETTE MARSH, SECRET AUTHOR

Georgie had not expected Mr. Aaron to actually bring in a contract for the second book. Nor had she expected him to write her a cheque for a book he hadn't yet read. But even more, she didn't expect the cheque to include funds above the advance of her last book. She hadn't even understood that she *could* earn more.

Was she an idiot for not realizing her book could make more than it already had? Charles had been forced to show her the contract, the reports of her books sales and promise her time and again that the numbers were accurate.

Georgette took a long, deep breath in and let it out slowly, clutching her handbag close to her body. That cheque—she shook her head. Tears were burning in her eyes to a level that made watching someone read her book seem like nothing. There was more than enough in that cheque to buy the wardrobe she dreamed of, furniture, *and* put more away.

Mr. Aaron walked her down to the street and made sure she got a black cab. She took it to the same bank location, made her deposit, and refilled her tea stash, buying her favourites and several more blends that called to her. She noticed a furniture store the next door over and ran out to the cabbie. "Will you stay a little longer?"

"Lady," he said, "you're on the clock. Do whatever you want."

She grinned and hurried back to the furniture shop. It was second-hand, but she had seen a set that had paused her in her tracks. Her head cocked outside the store as she glanced through the window.

There were two rounded, deep armchairs made of dark brown leather. They had brass buttons along the edges. Across the showroom was a deep cranberry sofa with rounded edges and buttons that added style and detail. There were two wooden chests that were cube shaped and of a height to be side tables. Georgette stared at them long enough that the salesman approached.

"Are you interested in these items, miss?"

She noted the miss when she'd been receiving ma'am for years, noted the way he frowned at her clothes. "I am indeed. I will need you to lower the price by twenty percent and delivery to Bard's Crook within the week." It was the racing for the train, Georgette thought. She'd felt like a character in a book and here she was channeling another character. Someone bold and gregarious.

The man blinked and laughed.

"I have ready money, sir, and I am prepared to leave if you are not willing to accept my offer."

"Perhaps," he started to adjust, but Georgette had listened to salesmen speak and knew that twenty percent was a good but reasonable negotiation price, and she really did hate haggling. She simply lifted her brow and waited.

"I prefer not to negotiate, sir. You may accept or decline my offer, but that is the only offer I will accept unless you'd like to take twenty-five percent off of the listed price?"

He laughed at her again and she nodded, heading towards the door of the shop.

"Wait!"

She turned and lifted a brow.

"What about..."

She turned and exited again. "Good day, sir!" Her heart was pounding with her sheer daring. She could hardly believe that she had been so bold.

It wasn't until the door closed behind her and she was crossing the street to the black cab when he came rushing out.

"I have a black cab running, so please don't think you can get me to adjust my offer."

Georgette stood staunchly, feeling very much like the heroine in a novel. It was *just* the sort of action of the woman who had run and caught the train. She wondered what her mother and grandmother would think of Georgette's behavior this year. She suspected her grandmother would cheer and her mother would be quietly shocked. She would, however, be proud.

Georgette arranged to have the furniture delivered and then hopped back into the black cab. She could hear Eunice already, telling her not to count her chickens before they hatch or buy her furniture before the book had even been read, but Georgette felt certain that Mr. Aaron would work with her on the book before he'd reject it outright. If he wasn't worried that she'd created a Chester Alvin on the lines Mr. Aaron had placed in her head, then Georgette wasn't going to worry that he'd try to get out of the contract that he'd so clearly explained to her.

She could tell herself she wasn't going to worry about it, but she already was. She had purchased furniture with money that Charles had given her for her work, but he *hadn't* read the book. Perhaps the first book was an anomaly. Perhaps she had just made a very costly mistake. Perhaps she was a greedy minx who'd decided to spend money she should have waited to confirm.

Georgette shook her head to escape the thoughts. She should tell Eunice to make a chicken dinner as soon as she was well. They'd roast that evil hen and never, ever keep chickens again. Miss Hallowton, the librarian, kept chickens and sold eggs. They purchased extra eggs from her often enough, but now they'd simply purchase eggs from her permanently.

Georgette grinned at the passing countryside, and her smile didn't fade until she reached home. The lively stream that ran through the town was bursting with the autumn rains, and Georgette decided to take the walk along the path rather than return directly home. Her packages of teas were no burden.

As she walked she caught sight of a cardboard box on the side of the stream. Georgette frowned deeply. She loved this stream. That someone would throw a box near here, the most beautiful part of Bard's Crook, upset her. She was nearly stomping to the box, but her mask was falling back into place, and Miss Georgette Dorothy Marsh didn't stomp.

When she had nearly reached the box, she heard the yip. It was followed by another and another and then a high-pitched whine.

"Oh, no!" She dropped to her knees, noting the soggy bottom of the box that had been washed onto the stream bank. A series of yips started up again as she pulled one puppy after another out of the box until there were four shivering, wriggling puppies in her lap. She took off her coat, wrapping the little pups inside. They looked a lot like a French bulldog, which had her running through the possibility of who might have tried to drown well-bred puppies, or any puppies, in her favourite stream.

If the fiend had succeeded, children could have found the tiny little bodies! She pulled them close to her and pushed herself to her feet. Georgette's leisurely ramble home ended with the shivering, muddy puppies. She hurried across the green, and in her haste, bumped into another person when she turned onto the lane.

"Oh, my," a girl said. "I am so sorry!"

Georgette looked up from her bundle of puppies. She was too angry from the attempted drowning and too exulted from selling her second book and buying furniture to keep her mask firmly in place. "Oh, hello."

Georgette adjusted her bundle of puppies and tea as the girl reached out and took the brown paper package from the teashop. She was incredibly lovely with dark chestnut hair, big blue eyes, and full pink lips. She looked as though she were just out of school with a clear, excited gaze. "You do look burdened. Are those puppies?"

"They are."

"Are they wet?"

"Someone tried to drown them." Georgette nearly snarled but recalled at the last moment who she was supposed to be in Bard's Crook.

"Oh! That does make me angry." The girl took one of the puppies from Georgette. "Who would try to drown such an angel?" She kissed the muddy nose. "Let me help you get them home."

"I don't know you," Georgette said.

"And you know everyone?"

"Well, yes," Georgette said. "This is Bard's Crook. Everyone knows everyone. All the details of their lives, everything."

They both paused as they saw a group of people across the green. Two of them were shouting at each other.

"Do you know who they are?" the girl whispered.

"I do." Georgette eyed the group. Poor Harriet Lawrence was standing at a distance from the others. Mr. Evans was shouting directly into Bertrand Lawrence's face as Mr. Smith looked uncomfortably on.

She had done this, she thought. She'd only linked the stories of how they treated their wives. She had wanted to show that Mr. Lawrence was as cruel and horrible as Mr. Evans. Georgette wasn't sure he abused his wife with more than words, but she thought he might. It was no secret that Mr. Evans did.

One of the puppies yipped. "We should go." Georgette hurried away and glanced back until the girl rushed to catch up.

"That was..." The girl shook her head. "I'm sorry. It's none of my business."

Georgette bit her lip tightly. There was no relationship between Mrs. Evans and Mr. Lawrence. Georgette had created that. She had done all of this, and she'd done it again with the new book. She'd been so happy about the furniture. She'd have pressed her fingers to her temple and bemoaned what she'd done, but not with a girl barely out of school watching and a pile of freezing puppies in her arms.

Georgie forced herself away from the argument. There were puppies to take care of, and that she knew she could do.

"Do you know who tried to kill these puppies?" the girl asked. "I think we should enact vengeance." The girl grinned winningly as they turned onto Georgette's lane.

Georgie couldn't think of vengeance with the confrontation between Mr. Evans and Mr. Lawrence still so fresh in her mind. Everything felt off and she was uncomfortable in her own skin. Why was she letting this girl intrude? Where was the mask she normally wore? Was it just that she was angry or that she needed help to get both the puppies and her things home? Georgette stretched her neck as they walked, wondering if she was finally moving beyond being Bard's Crook superfluous female.

"What is your name?" Georgette asked the girl instead as they walked up to the front porch. "Who are you?"

"Oh, my great aunt lives here—Mrs. Parker. Usually she comes to visit us, but this time it was decided I visit her. I wanted to stay with a friend for a few days, and my family was already leaving on a steamship, so I had to choose. I picked my friend and Aunt Parker. Father exchanged my ticket and let me have the money for a new wardrobe which was all the more desirable, though I think I quite disappointed him."

Georgette led the girl into her house. Marian Parker was her name, and she was eighteen, but she was bemoaning the choice to come to Bard's Crook for a week already. "I do love Aunt Parker, of course, but with Father and my little sister around, I never got the full focus of her attention before. It's—well—it's like I am seven years old again and having to ask before I add sugar to my tea!"

Georgette laughed. She left the girl in the bath with the puppies for a moment to grab several towels while Marian cooed over them with happiness. The pressing needs of Eunice and the puppies had Georgette setting aside manners for what needed to be done right away.

"I'm sorry," Georgette said. "I just...Eunice—"

"Don't worry about it," Marian replied. "I'll warm up the pups, you check on your maid, and then we'll make sure these little furry babies are all right."

Georgette hurried into Eunice's room, found her sleeping and refilled the water pitcher before pulling up the covers. "What have I done?" she asked the sleeping maid, but she had to whisper, so she didn't wake the poor woman.

Georgette returned to help wash the puppies with Marian, rubbing them until they were warm and lively again.

"Are you going to keep all of them?" Marian asked Georgette who shrugged. Two of the puppies were mostly white with grey patches. The other two were nearly all grey with white patches.

"I don't know," Georgette answered.

"I love this one," Marian said, holding up one of the mostly grey puppies. "May I have him? It's the only boy."

"You may," Georgette told her. "If you promised me that your Aunt Parker or your parents won't hunt me down later."

"No," Marian said. "I had a dog, and they know I've been looking for another. I don't mean to press you, but I feel like we are going to be friends."

"Does that mean you want to have supper with me? I can only make omelets."

"I do," Marian replied, "but I also want to be completely forceful and rude and suggest that you let me trim your hair."

CHAPTER 11

GEORGETTE MARSH, SECRET AUTHOR

Georgette stared into the mirror the next morning. "You," she told herself firmly, "let a girl you barely know cut your hair on the off-chance that she could turn a duck into a swan."

Georgette washed her face and adjusted her dress.

"Miss Georgie!" Eunice called from outside the bedroom as Georgette placed her shoes on her feet. "What is this in my kitchen? My girl, have you gone mad? Three puppies."

"There were four," Georgette said brightly as she left her room, and she wound her arm through Eunice's. "My dear Eunice, I am glad to see you up and well."

"Four! Did we lose one?"

"I met Mrs. Parker's great niece after I *rescued* them, and she took one."

"Rescued?"

"Someone tried to drown them," Georgette said, knowing it would get a reaction from Eunice.

"What do you mean?"

"I found them in a cardboard box, wet and shivering, crying for help on the bank of the stream. I believe someone put them in the box, shoved it into the river and left. But the current carried the box to the side. They were wet, but I think they'll be all right. Don't you?"

"They're mixed," Eunice declared. "If I were a gambling woman, I'd guess they're the pups from that woman who lives towards the hill. She has those fancy French bulldogs, but these ones have a touch of pug in them, I think. Just enough to not be able to trace a good ancestry."

They had arrived into the kitchen, and Georgette knelt next to the box she had found for them, checking the puppies over. They should have remained with their mother longer, but they were just old enough to make it without her. She snuggled each of the dogs, giving them a bit of milk and bread and then turned to Eunice.

"Mr. Aaron bought my next book."

"Did he? I saw it in your bedroom. Has he even read it?"

"He says he wants it regardless of the content."

"Did you tell him about *Mr. Alvin?*"

Georgette nodded, leaning forward to whisper as though they could have eavesdroppers in their house. "I didn't realize *The Chronicles of Harper's Bend* would cause so much trouble." She felt as though she were speaking to a confessor in that moment. "I never thought anyone would really read it when I sold it. I don't think I even expected it to sell at all and when it did, I never imagined anyone I *know* would read it. I never imagined that it would cause Mr. Thornton and Mr. Lawrence to attacked Mr. Aaron in his office, even if only verbally. And Mr. Evans…"

Eunice glanced at Georgette and then back to the stove. "Come now. Shall we have eggs and bacon?"

Georgette nodded and left the woman to her cooking while Georgette herself cleaned up the puppies and took them outside. She'd never had dogs before and the three little ladies she'd rescued seemed to need very proper names, she thought.

Her mind flicked to her new book as she played with the little dogs until breakfast was ready. She went to the bath to wash her hands and then to the table as Eunice carried out the food. As they ate, Georgette described the ordered furniture and watched the maid's gaze alight with interest.

"You must have been very well paid this time."

"It was quite a bit more for the second book, and I also received royalties. The first chronicles sold so many that I've earned even more money!"

"You need a new dress, Miss Georgie. You could do with several."

Georgette grinned as she admitted she intended to go to Marian's friend in London and order like mad.

Eunice snorted and left the table, saying over her shoulder, "Get a sturdy skirt or two to go with whatever fripperies you purchase."

Georgette finished her breakfast more slowly and lingered over her tea. It had occurred to her that she may well find herself doing quite well if she kept writing books. Mr. Lawrence, after all, kept his household with his books. She never expected to do as well as he did.

She sat down at her favourite desk in the parlor and began to work. Eunice had promised proper sandwiches and cakes for tea, so Georgette turned her mind to writing and taking the puppies out. As the day wore on, the mostly grey puppy received the name Dorcas. She was such a staid old thing for being a puppy that Georgette felt the dog had already become a little old lady, or she was doing poorly from her near-death.

When Georgette paused for fresh tea and a short ramble in the garden, the puppy with the gray ear and leg was named Beatrice. "I shall of course," Georgette told the dog, "call you Bea for short."

The dog looked up at her with adoring dark eyes and then nuzzled into Georgie's neck before wriggling to chase leaves that were blowing about the garden. It took until just before tea when Georgette expected Mr. Aaron to arrive for the name of the final puppy to occur to her. This one was the liveliest of the bunch and quite funny with what looked like a patch over her eye and a beauty mark on the left of her nose.

"Oh, Susan!" Georgette said as the dog nibbled at Georgette's new-to-her shoes. She laughed at the sound of it. "Oh, Susan! That is fun to say. Susan, dear, do stop chewing my shoes."

"And who is Susan?"

Georgette spun to find Mr. Aaron on the other side of the fence in a much more casual attire. He wore a collared shirt, a knit jumper, and brown tweed slacks.

"Hullo." She pressed her hand to her chest. "I didn't think you'd be here yet."

"Did I scare you?"

"Only a little," she confessed, "as nothing exciting happens in Bard's Crook outside of bad tea served at card parties, children bribed to be good with sweets, and this mad author writing people's secrets and combining it with scandalous fiction."

Mr. Aaron laughed and opened the gate. "And who is Susan?"

"This little lady," Georgette lifted the puppy while the other two came tripping over. "This is Dorcas. She's our staid miss. This one here is Beatrice, Bea for short."

"Ah, confidants."

"Well, not yet," Georgette said with a grin, smiling mostly because of the puppies. Inside her mind, she was telling herself not to worry over her book that she liked it better than the last, but she didn't really believe in herself. Her grin was mostly a lie while she worried he would hate it, demand back the cheque she had already deposited and partially spent on furniture.

Mr. Aaron insisted on reading the book right away though he did it with quite a charming grin, crinkles around the corners of his eyes and a delighted acceptance of a plate of sandwiches and biscuits along with a pot of tea. All the while Georgette paced the kitchen.

"If he hates it," she told Eunice, "we shall have to cancel the furniture order."

"You shouldn't have bought them until you knew for certain."

"They were used, Eunice. So much cheaper and *just* what I wanted."

Eunice shook her head and kneaded the bread for dinner.

"I suppose you're right."

"I am."

Georgette shot her maid a look that was entirely without effect. These, Georgette thought, were the consequences of living with a woman who had changed her nappies, taught her to eat at the table, and made sure Georgette knew how to read. She grinned at the woman, who lifted a brow in return.

"I suppose it's too late now, so we'll just have to see how it plays out."

Georgette topped off her tea, added a large dollop of cream, and nodded vigorously. "Just so."

Mr. Aaron left where he'd been reading two hours later and approached Georgette, who was writing in the dining room. She'd normally have remained at her writing desk, but she hadn't wanted to be in the same room as Mr. Aaron read.

"It was delightful," he told her cheerily. "No need to worry, my dear. You're an excellent writer, and I think it'll do even better than the first. We'll have to name it something, so people know that they don't *have* to read the first one."

She stared at him, blinking a little stupidly. His charming grin and the happy look on his face, the way he rubbed his hands together as though he were about to partake a warm cookie.

"You don't hate me?"

Mr. Aaron shook his head and grinned. "You are quite clever. It shocks me that your neighbors haven't guessed you wrote it. "

"They don't see me as clever, and I'm grateful they haven't realized it was me," she said. "I should very much like to avoid being strung up."

"Surely they can't be that angry? Would you like to walk? Would it be safe or do we risk the aggressive Mr. Thornton and Mr. Lawrence?"

"Safe enough. Mr. Thornton spends every afternoon in his office, smoking and going about his business. Mr. Lawrence writes late and still gets up early, but he naps in the afternoons after tea."

"You do note all the details, don't you?" Mr. Aaron's gaze crinkled down at her, and she looked away, uncertain of how to explain. She did, however, have another thought.

"We shall need a ready lie if anyone asks," she suggested.

"What if I am here as a representative of some relative? That way you can claim that your increased fortunes come from them rather than your writing." Either he was quite clever or he'd given the matter some thought.

"Oh yes," Georgette said. "I fear not all of my subjects have enjoyed what I've done to them as you have," she confessed as they walked. "If they find out it was me who wrote these things, I shall have to leave Bard's Crook."

"Oh?" He read the something in her tone that said she was upset. "What is happening now?"

"I'll have to explain the backstory of their lives first." Georgette spoke of Mrs. Evans and Mrs. Lawrence, telling all of the little signs she'd seen that made her feel certain that the neighbor women weren't being treated as they should be.

"I thought that their stories should be intertwined in my book, since they had similar—but also very different—problems. I wound them together with Theodora—the doctor's wife. She chose so much better than her friends. In reality, Mrs. Evans does spend quite a bit of time with Theodora. And Theodora and Harriet—that's Mrs. Lawrence—are very good friends.

"There is, however, minimal contact between Harriet and Mrs. Evans. I think Mr. Evans approves of Theodora. She's so sweet. She's clever, but she very rarely shows her cleverness around Mr. Evans, so he just sees the doctor's wife and the mother. Harriet, on the other hand, is quite clever all the time. She's independent too, despite the way Mr. Lawrence acts towards all women. But he's not so bad as to refuse Mrs. Lawrence her friends and activities."

"So you like him?" Charles asked, and Georgette shook her head emphatically. They had reached the stream again and a part of Georgette was afraid to look and find that she'd missed a puppy and it hadn't survived. Another part of her was on the lookout for any person who dared to put another litter of puppies or kittens in the stream again.

"I think it must be worse to live with him. He makes you doubt yourself. Everything is contempt with him. If he thinks he can—" Her head tilted and her voice came to a complete stop. There was something on the stream bank again. "Is that more puppies?" She wanted it to be. Live, muddy, wriggling puppies. Oh, she wanted it to be, but she knew it wasn't.

Charles followed her gaze and then pulled her behind him as though there were some threat. There wasn't. The threat was long past and never directed towards Georgette.

"No," Charles told her, glancing back at her. "Stay here." He rushed to the stream, pulling the rest of the object out of the water. If she saw it as an object, maybe she could pretend as though it hadn't happened. As though it was as much fiction as the end of her books, but no. No.

Charles pulled the body out of the water and flipped it over. He looked up at Georgette, who met his gaze, dark with the weight of what he was seeing.

A man. A dead man. In Bard's Crook where nothing ever happened.

"Go for the doctor and the police," Charles ordered and Georgette spun.

CHAPTER 12

"Dr. Wilkes," Georgette called, having caught sight of him in the distance. "Oh, Dr. Wilkes, please stop."

He did stop and turn, but he looked back over his shoulder again and again as she raced towards him. He clearly had somewhere to be and was probably late, given that he often was late. It was something of a joke, so much so she'd made him late to every appointment in her book. He was too nice, and all of Bard's Crook took advantage of him.

"Miss Marsh," he said gently, "I have been requested. I've heard Eunice is unwell. I need to see Justice Kensington, but I will try to see her later."

"Eunice is fine." She grabbed his wrist to stop him from moving on as she caught her breath. "There's a body!"

His head jerked towards her and then she saw that doubt filter in. Georgette Marsh, the quiet wallflower everyone assumed was too stupid to recognize what was happening around her. It had served her well in writing her book, but she found that the category she had been placed in had become stifling.

"Oh!" Georgette dug her fingers in before he turned on her. "There is a body," she said precisely, "in the stream. I believe he cannot be saved, but you are required."

Whatever his doubts, he was too kind to speak them, and it was too important if she wasn't wrong. "Where?"

"Down by the bend, just out of the wood. Please! Please hurry."

Dr. Wilkes nodded. She had never realized that he, too, saw her as the cipher who was too stupid to carry on. "I'll go that way, shall I?"

"Oh!" She barely kept herself from stomping her foot. She was *not* a child and would *not* allow her village to make her feel like one. Instead, she snapped, perhaps for the first time, not bothering to hide her thoughts. "Yes, by the bend. A dead man. You're needed. A Mr. Charles Aaron is with the body."

Mr. Wilkes blinked and glanced at her again. Suddenly, her story was valid because of Mr. Aaron. Oh, to be a man! Heard simply by the virtue of one's sex. Georgette watched him go, ensuring he wasn't merely placating her and heading towards his appointment, but she knew he wouldn't promise one thing and do another.

When she was certain he was rushing towards the stream, she hurried through the village, bypassing Mrs. Thornton, Miss Hallowton, and Mr. Evans to find the sole constable of Bard's Crook, Andy Daisy. Yet again, she had to repeat herself and even after she had, the police officer only went to examine the body because she refused to leave him until he did so.

He went begrudgingly and she had to prompt him along the way until they finally joined Charles, Dr. Wilkes, and the herbalist—Mr. Hadley. Where *had* he come from?

The body, Georgette saw when she returned, was Mr. Bertrand Lawrence. She almost couldn't process what she was seeing. It was a face she knew, but it was all wrong. It was a person she hadn't liked, but she never wanted to see dead. *Why* was he dead? The stream wasn't deep enough that someone as able as Mr. Lawrence would fall in and die.

"Did he fall?" Georgette asked as she stepped closer to Charles and Mr. Hadley, who were watching but keeping out of the way of Dr. Wilkes. Both men had muddy shoes and hands as though they'd help to move the body, and she saw that Mr. Lawrence was entirely out of the water.

"I am afraid not," Dr. Wilkes replied to her question, but he was speaking to the policeman. "There's quite a wound on the back of the head and that—"

Dr. Wilkes' foot nudged the dead man's leg, which twisted in the water, stirring the current. Both Georgette and the policeman, Andy Daisy, froze as a wooden shape very much like a cricket bat shifted on the other side of the body. It was bloodied, muddied, and wet.

She blinked rapidly, holding her mouth with one hand and her stomach with her other. This was *all* her fault. Tears burned heavily in her eyes and she turned away. A moment later, an arm wrapped around her and patted her back. She assumed it was Mr. Aaron since he was her friend, until she heard from a distinctly different voice. "There, there."

Georgette jerked back and saw Mr. Hadley. "I—I'm sorry."

"It's a terrible thing to lose a vital man like Mr. Lawrence," Mr. Hadley told her pedantically "It's rather worse when someone decided he needed to go."

Georgette nodded frantically as Mr. Aaron pressed a handkerchief into her hands. She stepped away from them both, wrapping her arms around her waist. She had little doubt that Mr. Aaron knew the direction of her thoughts.

"What are you doing out here? Did you see anyone about?" Officer Daisy asked Mr. Hadley.

Mr. Hadley gestured towards a basket. "I was gathering. I'm an herbalist, you'll recall. I saw Mr. Smith gathering mushrooms, and I saw Mr. Evans just as I entered the wood."

He paused, his gaze to the side, and the policeman said, "Come now, out with it."

"I—well...I—" He closed his eyes. "I saw Mrs. Lawrence walking with Mr. Lawrence along the stream. They were arguing. She seemed quite upset. Crying and the like."

The like? Georgette wanted to scoff. Of course she was crying. When Mr. Lawrence decided to be cruel, he did it so well that anyone would crumple, let alone a woman who had to sleep in the same bed.

Dr. Wilkes closed his eyes next as he digested what the presence of poor Mrs. Lawrence meant. Harriet Lawrence was, by far, his wife's closest friend. Georgette had envied their friendship for years.

Before they convicted Harriet in their heads, Georgette felt something must be said. "Mr. Lawrence has made me cry. He's made Theodora cry. He's driven Mrs. Thornton into a rage where she threw her teacup at him. He had Mrs. Baker calling him an out and out cad and ordering him to never speak to her privately again. If any woman has been driven to tears by *that* man, it was Mrs. Lawrence. Time and again, I am sure. I have witnessed multiple occasions myself. I feel confident that if she didn't murder him the last one hundred times, we can at least assume she isn't inherently murderous."

"You women can be so emotional," Officer Daisy replied. He glanced at the other men for support.

Georgette's gaze narrowed, and she demanded, "Dr. Wilkes! How many times have you made Theodora weep?"

He cleared his throat. "More than I'd like, Miss Marsh."

"And have you ever feared for your life, even at her most emotional?"

He shook his head. "Simmer down, little lady. No one has assumed that Mrs. Lawrence is a killer simply because her husband—who we all struggled with at times—made her weep."

"See that you don't convict her in your minds unfairly," Georgette ordered, shocked to find her hands were clenched into fists at her sides. "I assure you all that women may be capable of murder, but men murder *far more often* and for *far less reason.*"

"Any court will need proof beyond a weeping woman," Charles told Georgette. "You're right to leap to her defense. It is far more likely to be a man than his poor wife who murdered this fellow. Especially with that instrument, I imagine."

"We'll need an auto to move the body," Officer Daisy told Dr. Wilkes.

"We can use mine," Dr. Wilkes said. "It won't be the first time it has moved a body." He sighed and added, "I'm sure it won't be the last time."

They both glanced towards the group of three watching them.

"We'll need you to retrieve the auto." Dr. Wilkes to Mr. Hadley. "Tell Theodora I sent for it without any details."

Mr. Hadley blushed rather brilliantly. "I'm afraid I don't drive."

The policeman and Dr. Wilkes glanced at each other. Before the doctor could go for the auto himself, Mr. Aaron said, "I am able to drive. If Miss Marsh will show me the way, I would be happy to retrieve your auto. I wonder if I might use your telephone? I need to let my office know where I am."

"We're not quite ready for you to leave Bard's Crook," Officer Daisy said quickly. "Why are you here anyway?"

"I had paperwork for Miss Marsh regarding a recent beneficial arrangement. I'm Aaron of Aaron and Luther in London." Charles held out his hands placatingly. "Of course I'll stay, Officer Daisy. It's that very reason that I'd like to contact my office. I have no intention of leaving your village when I might have information that could be needed and as long as I can find a place to stay."

Miss Marsh glanced at him. "Miss Hallowton keeps boarders."

"Miss Hallowton can't keep a stranger after a murder!" Mr. Hadley squeaked. He was still red from admitting to not being able to drive, but his flush deepened as he glanced at Mr. Aaron and shook his head emphatically.

"Mr. Aaron was in my home with the paperwork today," Georgette snapped in an entirely uncharacteristic manner. "And then we left at the same time when he wanted to stretch his legs before returning to London. When did you see Mr. Lawrence alive?"

Mr. Hadley stumbled. "I—well, it must have been right around tea time or so."

"Mr. Aaron arrived at my house just after 1:00pm and stayed through tea time."

Their doubting glances made her so angry her ears felt as though they'd been set on fire. "Eunice will say the same."

"Of course, of course," Dr. Wilkes said and Constable Daisy nodded.

"Of course," Georgette said, shooting an exasperated look to Charles, who had a bit of a smile about the edges of his mouth. Her gaze narrowed on him, and she thought the only reason he wasn't laughing was because of the body and the seriousness of what they were facing.

A murder. One of Georgette's few friends as a suspect. A book that may well have caused this crime, and an author who needed to see justice attained.

$\mathscr{G}$eorgette took a long, deep breath in as Mr. Aaron drove Dr. Wilkes's auto away toward the stream. Theodora glanced at Georgette. The look on Theodora's face said that Georgette should leave and allow Theodora to tell her friend that her husband had died. It was a moment to blink stupidly and linger.

"Well," Theodora said, "the weather is nice."

Georgette smiled vaguely.

"I do think it would be better for Harriet to learn of her husband's death from me," Theodora said carefully.

"I think so too," Georgette agreed. "I'll go with you."

Theodora shook her head as she squeezed Georgette's hand. "I will do this. You don't have to be there."

"I should be there," Georgette said sweetly with that same stupid vague smile. "I think that Harriet could use the kindness and support to know that she isn't alone in this time of sorrow. It's important to surround her in love."

Theodora huffed in frustration and Georgette pretended to not see it. It wasn't as though Georgette could say, "Well, you see, I wrote the book that may well have caused this death. And in writing it, I feel responsible to an extent for Mr. Lawrence's death. But since no one is asking for my thoughts, I'll admit to myself I see his death as a crime but no great loss. However, it would be a travesty beyond belief if Harriet were blamed for his murder. It was entirely too true that if he'd married a lesser woman, she'd have murdered him long ago. Harriet should be praised not punished."

Georgette didn't speak her mind, but neither did she leave. Theodora wasn't quite cruel enough to refuse to let Georgette come, so they walked together to the Lawrence house and knocked. The Lawrences were well off enough to have help and the woman who opened the door greeted them with abruptness. "Mrs. Lawrence is not at home."

"It's rather important that we speak with her," Theodora told the woman.

"I'm sorry," she replied. "Mrs. Lawrence was very specific that she is not at home."

"And I am sorry," Theodora replied, stubbornly, "but I am *not* leaving without speaking to Harriet. There has been an...incident—and it's necessary that I speak with her."

The woman gestured reluctantly to the parlor, leaving the door open, and then disappeared up the stairs. A few minutes later, Harriet Lawrence appeared. She tried to smile but both Georgette and Theodora glanced away. There was quite a large, red mark on her face that was fading into a bruise.

"Oh, Harriet," Theodora said gently. "Oh no."

"It'll be all right," Harriet said. "Bertrand already apologized profusely. It'll fade. It...is what it is. Brave face forward and all that."

Georgette wanted to reach out and take Harriet's hand, but Georgie knew too well that her touch wouldn't be welcome. Instead, she pressed her fingers over her mouth.

"It's all right, Miss Marsh," Harriet said as kindly. "I know it's hard to be alone, but there are positives, aren't there?"

The tears that had threatened to fall when she and Charles had found the body and then tried to break free when she realized Lawrence had been murdered finally did break free. Georgette reached out and grasped Harriet's hand, squeezing. She would have told Harriet of her loss, but it would come better from Theodora, so instead Georgie shot Theodora a commanding look.

"Harriet," Theodora said so quietly, so gently that Harriet looked up in alarm. "It's Mr. Lawrence. He's…he's died."

Harriet shook her head slightly over and over again. It went on for too long, and it was clear that Harriet *understood* what she'd heard but she couldn't believe it. Finally she said, "He—he—he was fine. He was *fine.*"

"I'm sorry." Theodora's statement was cautious, almost a question.

"It—it—*is* it true?" Harriet's voice cracked, and her eyes were so fixed on Theodora's face that Georgette felt that she could read into the expression a sense of hope. Was that what Georgette wanted for Harriet or was it what the new widow actually felt? Georgette knew it wasn't fair to assume that Harriet was glad that her husband was dead simply because Georgette was glad that Harriet was freed from his tyranny.

"He was murdered, they think." Theodora's voice was still in that soft, gentle tone, telling poor Harriet what Charles and Georgette had explained when they'd arrived for the auto.

"Murdered?" Harriet frowned deeply, pressing her hand to her face with a wince.

"Murdered," Theodora repeated.

"But how can that be? How? Was he…was he shot? Was he stabbed? How can you say that he was murdered?"

Georgette glanced at Theodora. Charles and Georgette hadn't shared what they knew about Lawrence's death beyond the fact that it had been suspected murder. She bit her lip and then admitted, "I—I'm not sure what I can say."

Harriet stared at Georgette and then asked, "How can you keep it from me?"

"You have to know you're a suspect," Georgette said very carefully. "You were the last person seen with him. I believe if I were to tell you what I know in advance of the constable or whoever investigates, I could be sullying what they're up to."

Theodora's jaw dropped and the two friends glanced at each other, leaving Georgette entirely out. It wasn't an unfamiliar sensation. What was unfamiliar is that Georgette *cared* for once. She'd always liked both women. She'd always admired them and wished to be better friends with them. Never had it been illustrated more clearly to her that she wasn't one of them. Not really.

She scolded herself a moment later as Harriet wept into Theodora's shoulder. The woman who deserved sympathy at the moment was Harriet, and Georgette should stop feeling sorry for herself.

"Did you see anyone after you left your husband?" Georgette asked.

"I was trying to hide my face," Harriet said between sniffles.

"Can you think of anything, anything at all that could help show that it wasn't you who killed your husband?"

"If I'd have killed my husband," Harriet said calmly, "I'd have been far cleverer about it and no one would have suspected me."

Georgette stared at the woman, and their gazes met. Harriet met Georgette's gaze without shame. She had little doubt after meeting that gaze that Harriet had at least considered murder to escape her life. Yes, Georgette thought, Harriet was innocent. Georgette believed that statement in its entirety. If Harriet had done the crime, she'd never have been suspected.

CHAPTER 14

CHARLES AARON, PUBLISHER (EARLIER)

"Detective Inspector Joseph Aaron at Scotland Yard please," Charles said in a hushed voice. "Tell him that it is Charles." It took a while to be connected to Scotland Yard and even longer for Joseph to be brought to the telephone. By the time Charles spoke with his nephew, he was feeling quite the value of his secretary Mr. Schmitt, who was the one who had to handle this inane wait.

"Charles?" the tinny voice asked.

Charles considered for a moment as to how to say what needed to be said without giving the possible eavesdropper connecting the line fodder for gossip. "Do you remember that story I told you at dinner yesterday?"

"The one about the—?"

"Yes," Charles said, cutting in before Joseph finished, but yes—the one about the book and Miss Marsh, and the outraged citizens of Bard's Crook who ended up in Charles's office. The night before, Joseph had laughed over the idea of a quiet little mouse sending the local lions into a rage and then blinking innocent eyes while they

86

roared, with the author in sight. Joseph had nearly choked on his steak and potatoes. "I came down to Bard's Crook today and one of yesterday's visitors to my office was discovered in a manner that will cause a call to the yard today."

"To the yard?" Joseph demanded. "For help? For *our* help?"

"Indeed," Charles agreed. "There have been unforeseen consequences of the manner you normally deal with to the document and situation I told you about." He was fortunate that his nephew was quick to understand the need for vagueness.

"What the devil?" Joseph choked.

"Indeed," Charles sighed. "I don't know how things work around where you are, but perhaps someone who would assist me in my goal of keeping certain things—ah—secret could be assigned, if that's possible."

"Seems all the more important if my work is necessary." Joseph's tinny voice still conveyed the worry that gnawed at Charles. He felt a rush of relief at Joseph's understanding. His nephew would help Charles protect Miss Marsh.

"Exactly my point," Charles agreed. "Someone I feel responsible for who is at risk. Whatever you can do."

"I'll see what I *can* do." Joseph coughed and then cleared his throat. "Nothing can be done until the call comes in requesting help."

"There's no reason to believe what was written was factual," he informed Joseph. "When the person who committed the deed realizes that, they may well go hunting."

"I understand. Regardless of who is assigned, I'll speak to them."

"Thank you. I'll be staying here until I'm sure that my subject is secure."

"I understand. I'll do what I can."

Charles ended the call and glanced around the office, hoping he'd been vague enough. It seemed that no one had been around while he was speaking to his nephew, but no doubt, Mrs. Wilkes was carefully questioning Georgette over what she knew. Charles hadn't missed the utter shock on the doctor's wife face when she took in the sight of Miss Marsh with a gentlemen. When they had explained there had been an accident and Miss Marsh had been engaged to show Charles the way to retrieve the auto, acceptance crossed Mrs. Wilkes's face instead.

The gentlemen had been the same when they learned that Miss Marsh had been walking with Charles. It wasn't protectiveness for a local. Instead, they couldn't imagine her capable of interesting anyone. Charles shook his head as he adjusted his jumper. They really were blind to what was happening around them.

Despite their opinion of her, Miss Marsh liked the Wilkes. It was clear given the way they were portrayed in the novels. Dr. Wilkes had seemed genuinely upset by Lawrence's death. Was that because of his wife's friendship with the victim's wife or for some other reason? If the wives were good friends, did that mean the men were good friends as well? How did it work when you were married?

He took the auto to the crime scene, deliberately going slowly to take in the town that Miss Marsh had described so perfectly. When he reached the body, he found several more men had arrived at the scene. Charles glanced around, looking for Mr. Thornton since the man could have recognized him. He wasn't there, so Charles risked getting out of the auto and approaching the gathering.

Mr. Hadley was still present, so Charles stepped next to him, hoping that Hadley's acceptance of his presence would be enough for the others.

"I can't believe this," a man said, staring down at the body, which had been covered with a jacket. "I can't believe that someone would kill Lawrence. *Why?*"

Charles watched them all. Several of the men glanced at the speaker and then back to the body as though they thought he was a bit dim. One man even snorted.

"What I want to know," Mr. Hadley said, "is whose cricket bat is that?"

"You boys just leave the detecting to the professionals," Officer Daisy warned, glaring around the group.

"We're not trying to edge in," said the man Charles had heard the others refer to as Smith. "We're just musing. It has to matter, doesn't it, whose cricket bat that was."

"I imagine," Dr. Wilkes told them with a bit of a scowl, "that it only matters whose bat it is, where it was kept, and how it was acquired. Because if it was one man's bat doesn't mean another man didn't use it. Which is why," he said with emphasis, "we leave it to the professionals. Officer Daisy will be calling in Scotland Yard who will track it all down."

"The yard? Can't we handle this ourselves?" Smith asked.

"Nope," Officer Daisy said. "And nope again boys. The last time there was murder around here, we called in the yard. It's what the higher-ups want unless it's clear cut who the killer is from the beginning. Those boys work these kinds of cases all the time. No shame in not having any experience tracking down a killer. No sense in letting pride get in the way of doing what's right for Lawrence."

"Isn't it probably the wife? Isn't that how it goes?" another man asked. "Think I read an article about that."

"It's the other way around," Dr. Wilkes said. "If a woman comes up dead, you start looking at the men in her life. Men are killers far more often than women."

"That's enough of that," Officer Daisy said. "We've got the pictures, we've got what we were able to find. We're going to move the body and call in the yard."

CHARLES WATCHED the other men load the body into the auto. There were quite a few suspicious looks sent his way, but he saw both Wilkes and Hadley look towards Charles and then explain his presence to the others. When loading was finished, Mr. Hadley, the herbalist, remained behind along with Mr. Smith.

"Saw you earlier," Mr. Hadley told Smith, who nodded.

"I saw you myself," Mr. Smith said.

The two of them eyed each other. Being in the wood and having seen Lawrence before he died made them both suspects.

"Mrs. Lawrence was with him when I saw him," Hadley offered.

Smith's jaw clenched, which struck Charles quite forcefully before the man glanced at him. "I saw her too. Can't imagine she killed her husband. Not that way."

"It's easy to slide a woman into a gentle and sweet category," Mr. Hadley said. "If we look to nature, we see species after species that are quite a bit more dangerous than the male."

"If we look to history," Mr. Smith shot back, "we see women by far more often the victim of a man's cruelty. There's absolutely no reason to believe that Mrs. Lawrence killed her husband. I saw her leaving the wood myself. Did she look upset? Yes. Not sure I would have looked so different after walking with the man. No need to turn him into a saint just because he's dead."

Smith smacked his hand against his thigh and snarled towards both Mr. Hadley and Charles before rushing into the wood.

"I've an extra room," Hadley told Charles. "I'd prefer you stayed with me rather than Miss Hallowton."

"I understand she takes boarders," Charles said.

"We don't know you," Hadley said a bit delicately and shoved his spectacles up his nose.

"The nature of boarders," Charles replied, "is that you do not know them. Of all your neighbors, I'm the one who has an alibi. Twice over with Eunice included, and given her fierceness, I think we must include her."

"Fierce? Eunice?"

Charles laughed. "Come now, Mr. Hadley. Let's be friends. I didn't kill Lawrence. Not only do I have an alibi, I have no reason to have killed him. I am concerned, however, Miss Marsh is a bit under my care due to our interests. I am in charge of this beneficial arrangement for her. Do I need to be concerned about her safety?"

Hadley laughed grimly and then admitted, "I wouldn't have thought that anyone would be in danger in Bard's Crook."

"Even with this recent uproar about that book?"

"Did Miss Marsh tell you about that?" Hadley adjusted his eyeglasses again and then sighed. "People were upset about that, and I can't blame them. That Jones fellow made Thornton a laughing stock with his will nonsense. Lawrence and Evans were linked together and have every reason to be angry. Made them both look like animals, really. Not sure that anyone took it seriously. It switched over to fiction. The librarian character took off adventuring, but she's still here, isn't she? That nonsense about Mrs. Baker hasn't happened. No need to get so upset about things."

"What about outside of the book? Did you know Mr. Lawrence well?"

Hadley shook his head. "Not sure anyone did really. He writes those books of his. Bit off, really. All about a woman's place and what to eat, ways to spend your time and cultivate your mind. Hogwash when you know the man. Saw him getting a pint every Saturday night, didn't I? Yet the book of his that I read suggested abandoning all alcohol. Talked about eating mostly vegetables and grains, and yet, every pint was delivered with fish and chips."

Charles brows lifted. "Was it a bit of an act for his books? Never actually espousing what he wrote?"

"Far as I could tell he didn't practice what he preached." Hadley glanced back with a scowl towards where the body had been discovered. "To be honest, I could see someone who had lived as he instructed killing him if they found out it was all lies. His recommendations fair remove the joy out of life."

Charles shook his head, making sure that he seemed as shocked as he was. It wouldn't be the first time someone preached a life that they didn't live, but he'd seen how shocking it was when people realized. He'd have thought that Georgette would have mocked that in her book. Did she not know the truth of his life? Or, perhaps instead, she hadn't bothered reading his books.

CHAPTER 15

GEORGETTE MARSH, SECRET AUTHOR

Georgette returned to her cottage after leaving Harriet to Theodora. She had stayed long enough to know that Harriet had left Lawrence in the wood to run home after he'd hit her, keeping her face down to avoid anyone seeing what her husband had done to her.

What shocked Georgette was the *shame* on Harriet's face. Why did she feel ashamed? Because her husband had hit her? Because she'd driven him to it? Did she feel like it was her fault, somehow, because he'd lashed out? This was one of the many times that Georgette wasn't sure and regretted her situation.

"Hello," Georgette called, as she opened her door. The puppies yipped from their box but there was no reply from Eunice. Georgette took the puppies out to the garden and found Marian with her puppy.

"Hello!" Marian gasped. "I *have* been hoping you'd come home soon." She made kissing noises and the puppy she'd brought home appeared from under the flowers and darted towards Susan, Dorcas, and Bea.

"Did you need to return the puppy?"

Marian grinned. "Oh no. Never try to take my little darling." Her gaze flicked over Georgette and the puppies. "You have color in your face. It does make you look quite nice. You know if you darkened your brows, wore a little rouge, and had a dress that complemented your coloring, you'd be rather pretty."

Georgette didn't bother to hide her snort, and Marian laughed at the expression on her face.

"These are things that I know," Marian told Georgie. "You can't be expected to shine when you wear clothes that would make my great aunt look dowdy. You should let me go to London with you and pick out a few things. I have a friend who works in a shop there. We'd set you right up with something that made you seem—I don't know—a century younger."

"Perhaps," Georgette said, feeling quite daring, "I shall take you up on that. I won't believe myself to be capable of being pretty, of course. But I do need a new dress and a few other things. My coat should have been laid to rest a few years ago." Georgie would have to scold herself thoroughly to not be pulled into buying clothes that would look ridiculous on someone of Georgette's age.

Marian clapped her hands. "Yes! Though I will convince you that you are as lovely as we all are. We are going to shop and play and you'll see. We shall take the early train down, shop, have a delightful tea, and catch the train back. If I go with you, my Aunt Parker will be far less likely to object. Now—" Marian's gaze moved over Georgette's face. "Did someone really die?"

Georgette stepped back a little and nibbled her bottom lip before she answered. "Mr. Lawrence died."

"*Was* he murdered?" Marian's hands were pressed to her stomach as though she might just sick up if Georgette gave the wrong answer.

She nodded once and Marian paled.

"Was it someone gone mad?" the girl demanded.

"They don't know who it was yet," Georgette said carefully. The guilt she felt for writing a book that led to murder was conflicting with her excitement to buy new clothes with the stylish Marian.

"Are you afraid?" the girl asked.

She was, but Georgette wasn't going to tell the girl that. She wasn't afraid because she thought whoever killed Lawrence was going to come after her specifically. She was afraid that whoever killed Lawrence would realize that she had written the book that had driven them to such a terrible crime.

"I don't think you need to be afraid," Georgette told Marian.

The girl was young, but she wasn't stupid. She had caught the reference to 'you.' "Why are you afraid?"

Georgette just smiled and shook her head. Her gaze caught Marian's, and Georgette realized that possibly for the first time ever, another woman was looking at her and not seeing the blank gaze she normally wore.

"I—it's hard to explain and probably silliness on my part. It is getting late, however, and with the death…"

"I should hurry home," Marian said. "Aunt Parker does treat me like I'm a little girl. If I'm out late after a death, she may well call up a search party."

"I'm sure it's because she loves you," Georgette said, as Marian leaned down and scooped up her puppy. Georgette did the same with Susan and Bea and made kissing noises for Dorcas, who followed behind.

When she reached the kitchen, she found Eunice just pulling chicken and potatoes from the oven. "Mr. Aaron came back while you were outside. He said to leave you be, and he'd wait."

Georgette washed her hands and ran her hands over her dress, trying to smooth it out before she returned to the parlor. Mr. Aaron was smoking his pipe near the fireplace where Eunice had started a merry little blaze. The sight of it reminded Georgette of her changed circumstances, and she was instantly happier despite the events of the day.

"Oh, Mr. Aaron, did this day really happen?"

His head tilted and he tapped his pipe before he spoke. "None of that now. It's Charles and Georgette."

She grinned at him. "Would you like to stay to dinner?"

"I should like to talk to you about this business. But perhaps after dinner?"

"I can't offer coffee or wine after supper since I'm afraid we're all out of the luxuries around here other than tea, but I did invest in rather a lot of exciting blends recently."

"Tea before all else?" he asked.

She nodded and then led him into the dining room where Eunice had already set two plates. They ate, chatting about train trips and London, and returned to the parlor where Eunice brought in a tea tray. She'd used the rose congou tea blend and added a plate of sweet biscuits.

"I can't imagine Miss Hallowton will be thrilled if you're late," Georgette told him.

"True enough, but let's take a few minutes to list out who I saw as suspects, and we'll discuss them rather quickly, shall we?"

Eunice paused in the doorway and Georgette called, "Come have a cuppa with us, Eunice. You'll know details we don't."

The maid hesitated, but she was more family than servant and nodded a moment later, bypassing the china for her favourite tea mug.

"Who are the suspects, do you think?" Georgie asked him.

"The wife, the Smith fellow, the herbalist, you & I—although we do cancel each other out, though I'm not sure they believe that yet. From the book, I imagine whoever Elle Ende and Mr. Ende are in Bard's Crook."

"I'd say no good came of that book," Eunice muttered, "but we're eating, aren't we? Drinking tea and having fires? If I were to make a list off of what I know of this town outside of that book, Mr. Smith would be at the top of my list."

"But why?" Georgette demanded. "Isn't he only concerned because Elle Ende, I mean, Eliza Evans—oh, my book and the double names! He's Eliza's brother. If I thought that Mr. Lawrence was trying to manipulate a sister into running away with him—"

"No, not that." Eunice shook her head. "He's been in love with Harriet Lawrence for years. Since they were children. If he read your book and realized what a terrible husband Lawrence was, well, he might just feel the need to put on his shining armor."

Georgette leaned forward. "Really?"

"They're a bit older than you, Miss Georgie. The dueling affections for Harriet Lawrence occurred while you were still at school."

Georgette glanced at Charles. "So the book would have shown Mr. Smith that his one-time love was married to a cruel man and triggered violence? What about Mrs. Evans?"

Eunice's head tilted. "I don't think that Mr. Smith cares as much about his sister as he does about Harriet Lawrence. His maid, Betty, says he walks past the Lawrence house every day when it's a clear day because Mrs. Lawrence will always be in the garden. He even got a dog as cover for why he goes that way. Never takes his children, just the dog."

"Is he married?" Charles asked.

"Widowed," Eunice and Georgette said in unison.

They glanced at each other and then Georgette shivered. "I don't think I'd like it if some person who thought he loved me was walking by my house every day."

"That's because despite how everyone sees you," Eunice said dryly, "you've never been stupid."

"Why do they see her like that?" Charles demanded.

"She's quiet," Eunice told him. "She's so busy watching, people don't realize she's making note of everything she sees and putting together the little details. They assume she's not thinking at all because none of them can stop talking."

Georgette shot them both quelling looks.

Eunice laughed. "Uh-oh, Mr. Aaron, you saw the real Georgette. Now you're one of us. We're a select club. Even the few folks Georgette likes have no idea about her."

"Marian does," Georgette announced. "Mrs. Henry Parker's granddaughter had almost all my secrets in moments."

"Well, she did meet you when you were angry. It takes a lot to make my girl angry, Mr. Aaron, but when she gets angry, she doesn't keep her mask on very well."

Mr. Aaron's brows rose and he contemplated Georgette while he lit his pipe. "Angry, were you?"

"Who drowns puppies? All you have to do is give them away! They were wet and cold and what if there was one I didn't find?"

He reached out and took her hand, squeezing it once. "For such a small dog as the mother must have been, Georgette, any more than four puppies is unlikely."

It didn't make her feel better entirely. She would be haunted by the idea of a puppy for a few more weeks until either one didn't turn up or she let it go. She reached down as Susan tripped over her foot and lifted the little dog onto her lap.

"So you believe it was Mr. Smith because of Mrs. Lawrence and not his sister," Charles stated.

Georgette glanced his way. His gaze was warm on her. It was like Eunice or Georgette's parents but different somehow. Georgette scratched her fingers by Susan's ears, completely uncomfortable.

"Who else could it be?" Charles asked the two women.

"My list?" Eunice asked. "Mr. Evans, who is controlling of his wife and mean as a snake, Mrs. Lawrence who is, perhaps, tired of being tormented by a man daily and treated as though she should be lucky that he isn't hurting her physically."

"He did today," Georgette said softly, that anger returning and leaving her flush with fury. "He hit her bad enough that her face was swollen and red. It hadn't even bruised yet. It was still swelling."

Charles cursed under his breath while Eunice shook her head, unsurprised. "It happens often enough."

"What?" Georgette demanded while Charles asked, "Does it?"

"It isn't just Evans who is as mean as a snake," Eunice said, glancing between them. "The two of you are innocents. A bachelor and a superfluous woman who haven't had to actually learn how to live with another."

"Georgette isn't superfluous," Charles argued. "She's a brilliant writer. When they look back at our generation, she'll be remembered and the rest of us will be forgotten."

Georgette laughed mockingly. "She's quoting a ladies magazine.

An editor wrote on how the superfluous woman should embrace the status of being extra and find joy in it."

"Doing things like writing books and creating your own possibilities."

"Just so," Georgette replied.

CHAPTER 16

*G*eorgette woke the next morning to Eunice knocking on the door and a note from Marian. It was nearly as excitable as the girl herself:

My dear Miss Marsh,

If there is ever a time when Aunt Parker will allow me to go to London with you, it is when there is a murderer afoot. I swear you'll love the results. Please say yes.

~Marian

Georgette tapped her fingers against her bed as she considered and then decided it might be just the thing. She wouldn't be needed by Scotland Yard until they arrived. If they arrived today, she wouldn't be at the top of the list of people to speak to. Not until the yard had talked to Dr. Wilkes about the body itself, Officer Daisy about the crime scene, Mr. Aaron on finding the body, and Mr. Smith and Mr. Hadley about what they'd seen in the wood and near the stream. Her word would amount to next to nothing because she was a woman. Though they were certain to speak with Mrs. Lawrence.

Georgette sniffed. "Be honest with yourself, my dear," she said aloud. "You want new clothes and you trust Marian more than you trust yourself to choose them." She hopped out of bed and wrapped her worn robe around her shoulders before hurrying to the bath. She ran a washcloth over her body and washed her face, then pulled her brush through her hair.

It was the hair, she acknowledged in the mirror. Her hair looked better than ever in her life, and Marian had cut it with shears in the kitchen. What could the girl do for Georgette with the capacity to buy clothes that were *meant* to look decent on Georgie? She knew she wasn't beautiful, but perhaps she didn't have to be so dowdy.

The two women met the early train to London. They hopped on and snuggled down into their coats as though they were escaping.

"I don't want to look too young."

"Of course not. You didn't just leave school." Marian patted Georgette's hand comfortingly.

"I need solid things that will last. I haven't been able to buy new clothes—ever really. I don't know that I can expect a new wardrobe every year."

"I understand completely." Marian grinned winningly. "Do you know what you would like?"

"Things that I can wear together, so they seem like I have more than I have."

"Every stylish woman's smart decision. May I recommend a black dress? A few skirts that you can wear with a few blouses? Perhaps a jumper or two and a coat?"

Georgette nodded and then nibbled her bottom lip. Marian laughed. "Are you nervous about shopping?"

"My dear Marian," Georgette said with a bit of a smile, "I cannot remember the last article of clothing that was new when I received it."

Marian winced for Georgette but shrugged it off. "Tell me about this murder instead. You know all the players? You know, my Aunt Parker was shocked when I said you were funny and clever. Why does she think you're a...blank slate?"

Georgette shrugged.

"Tell the truth, my friend." Marian grinned again and Georgette held out her hands to stop her questions.

"I'm just quiet."

The girl in the shop was one of those intensely clever folks who had a sharp haircut, red lips, and embroidery on the sleeves of her blouse. Her skirt was somehow both simple and elegant, and Georgette instantly knew she would look ridiculous in it, *especially* in Bard's Crook.

"You need something soft," Tara the shop girl said. "Pleats. A pretty blouse. Delicate. You have such pretty coloring with your soft skin and freckles. You should own that. Maybe something in rust, cream, greens, and blues."

Georgette felt as though she'd been spun in a circle by the time they left, but she had a new dark brown coat, a cloche, three blouses, three long skirts, and two dresses. Tara must have felt sorry for Georgette because the total cost was lower than Georgette expected, even with stockings, underthings, and slips.

The train ride back had Marian pestering Georgette once more about the murder.

"Who do you think killed that man?"

Georgette answered this time. "I think it was Mr. Evans."

"Why?" Marian demanded. "Because he's like the one whose wife left with the one like Mr. Lawrence in the book? I remember seeing them arguing."

Georgette nodded, biting her lip. The fun of shopping for new clothes had faded, and she was left with the guilt. In the grand scheme of the universe, had *she* done this? Did she ultimately become responsible for this death? Was it on her? Because she wanted new clothes?

"Do you think the author who wrote the book is responsible for this?"

Marian's head tilted. "The author didn't wield that cricket bat, Georgie."

Georgette nodded and glanced out the window.

"You know, I read it."

"Did you?" Georgette looked away from the window.

"It's clever and funny. It's full of heart."

Georgette smiled a little.

"Have you read it?"

Georgette met Marian's gaze and saw knowing in them.

"I have."

"Whoever killed Mr. Lawrence—if it was over that book—he or she is mad. The fault doesn't lay with the author. It lays with the killer. Who might strike again."

Georgette's gaze widened as she nibbled her bottom lip and ran her hand over her new cloche.

"You should be careful, Georgie."

Georgette nodded and the two of them fell silent as they met the gaze of a man across the aisle. They had been speaking low, so he hadn't heard them, and his gaze was fixed on Marian. She was lovely, Georgette thought. There was something about him that was familiar and it took Georgette a few minutes to recognize it. He had a dimple in his chin rather like Mr. Aaron's.

Georgette met his gaze and saw familiar dark eyes. Calling on a bit of daring, she asked, "Mr. Aaron?"

The man jerked and he frowned. "Do I know you?"

"I believe I know your relative. Charles Aaron?"

JOSEPH AARON, DETECTIVE INSPECTOR

Joseph nodded. His gaze flicked over her, thinking of his uncle's description. A mouse? Hardly. She was not the most beautiful woman he'd ever seen and the young lady across from her was shockingly beautiful, but she was no mouse.

"Could you be Georgette Marsh?"

She nodded.

"Special trip up to London?"

"There was a murder," the young lady told Joseph. "London seemed safer."

Joseph nodded, though he could argue that fact.

"But you know that," Miss Marsh said.

"I do."

"You were the phone call."

He smiled at her. "I was."

"And you're coming to Bard's Crook?" the young lady asked. "For the murder?"

He nodded.

"Is Mr. Aaron the man who was walking with you when the murder occurred?" the young lady asked Miss Marsh, who nodded. "He's connected to your secret, right. The Mr. Aaron you were walking with? Do we all know the secret?" The young lady glanced between the two of them, but her gaze lingered on Joseph longer.

"We all know the secret," Joseph said, smiling slightly.

"It needs to stay secret," she insisted, leaning forward. "Just in case this madman turns his focus to our friend."

"I would like to say that it isn't necessary," Joseph said and then looked at Miss Marsh. She had soft brown hair, soft eyes, too many freckles, and flushed cheeks, but she was pretty enough. Add writing clever books and Uncle Charles being the one who'd discovered her secrets? Joseph Aaron was making personal bets about this being his future aunt.

Protectiveness surged through him. Uncle Charles had seen Joseph and Robert through their childhood after their parents had died. He wasn't a second parent, but he was their family, their guardian, and the man who'd seen them settled into their lives. Joseph reached out and shook both women's hands. "This, my dear ladies, is a conspiracy of secrets. We'll keep this one about the—shall we call it the document?"

"Yes," the young lady said, grinning charmingly. "The document is very much like a spy thriller."

"Are you the one who read the book first?" Miss Marsh asked.

He shook his head. "My brother, Robert. I work for Scotland Yard. Detective Inspector Joseph Aaron," he belatedly introduced himself.

"And," he continued, "unlike a spy thriller, we aren't going to have anything further happen. Tell me everything."

The young lady, who introduced herself as Marian Parker and insisted he call her Marian, told the story with verve, listing out the three main suspects while Miss Marsh listened quietly and Joseph took notes.

"And you, Miss Marsh? Marian has her theories. What do you think?"

"I think all of the main suspects were in the wood when he died. Harriet makes sense. He slapped her. She might have picked up the cricket bat to defend herself. Except Eunice—that's my maid—says that Harriet gets slapped more often than any of us would have thought."

Miss Marsh glanced out the window. "Mr. Evans is controlling and obsessive with his wife and if he thought that she might leave him —he'd kill Mr. Lawrence in a moment."

"You feel guilty?" Joseph asked, studying her.

"The document," Miss Marsh snapped, her anger striking swift and hard and surprising, and nothing like a mouse. "It changed my life. It wasn't supposed to be read by the subjects. It wasn't supposed to be taken seriously. I didn't write—"

Marian cleared her throat and Miss Marsh glanced around. No one was listening, but it was probably a good idea to practice veiling their speech. Joseph approved when he saw she realized it.

"What was in there about Elle Ende," she continued quieter, "was my hope for anyone who is living like that, not her specifically. Don't you think the clues were there? That there were signs that La—the victim was a narcissistic bastard? I'll wager Harriet missed them because she didn't want to believe."

Miss Marsh obviously felt strongly about the matter and had given it a great deal of thought.

"Women need to read these stories so they avoid the same fate," she told Joseph. "Women need to be careful before they marry. It's so hard for women to divorce if the man doesn't let her. You can believe that Mr. Evans would fight it."

Marian's gaze widened and she searched her friend's face. "What are you trying to say?"

"You know, people feel sorry for me. Like that magazine that Eunice reads referring to women in my situation as the extra woman."

"There is nothing extra about you," Marian declared. "Don't be sad."

"Don't you see? I'm not. Sometimes, before I wrote the document, I dreamed about a man coming along and saving me. Like Mr. Collins for Charlotte Lucas."

"Oh!" Marian shuddered, taking Miss Marsh's hand. Joseph sat fixed in place, stunned at her admission.

"Collins was security," Miss Marsh told her. "He wasn't even cruel. He was awful, yes. For Charlotte—she couldn't save herself. A lot of time has passed since then. I can save myself. I did, even. It's not *me* people should feel sorry for. They think I'm somehow less because a man doesn't love me. They should feel sorry for Eliza, whose husband controls her every move, even who she can be friends with, and is often cruel. They should feel sorry for Harriet because it's better for her now that her husband is dead. If she didn't kill him, the day will arrive—not too far from now—where she'll be weeping out of sheer relief. Society feels sorry for me. But I feel sorry for them."

Marian leaned back, still holding her friend's hand, and glanced at Joseph. He stared in shock at the woman his uncle was falling in love with. He doubted Charles even realized where things were heading or how he was feeling. It was apparent to Joseph, however, just why his uncle was succumbing.

"Hear, hear," he said.

"Brava," Marian agreed. "I knew I liked you. Who knew behind the old coat and pile of freezing puppies was such an eloquent soul?"

"My uncle," Joseph answered. "Of course, my uncle."

Miss Marsh's only answer was a brilliant, hot, red blush.

CHAPTER 17

JOSEPH AARON, DETECTIVE INSPECTOR

Joseph found the local constable first and listened as the man told him what was known about the deceased and his death. His only suspect was the wife. In comparison, Miss Marsh had concisely put together possible motives and possible killers based off of what she knew.

"Do you have any reason to believe that anyone other than Mrs. Lawrence is the killer?" Joseph asked.

"Why would anyone other than his wife kill him?" Constable Daisy demanded. "I've known the Lawrences for years, like we all have. Who else would have a grudge against the man?"

"I understand there was a book causing some trouble here."

"How d'ya know that?" Constable Daisy demanded.

"Is it true?" Joseph asked, refusing to clarify. He was here because his chief agreed that if the murder were caused by the book, the author was in danger.

"It's true there's a bit of an uproar. Mrs. Thornton showed up at the station the other day and demanded I find the author and make him pay. Bunch of nonsense if you ask me."

"People are, however, upset by the contents of the book."

The constable bit back a reply and then ground out, "The *fiction* book. I'm not much of a book man myself, but people don't kill over fairy stories."

Joseph stretched his neck. "Did you speak to the wife?"

"Dr. Wilkes put her to bed with a sleeping draught. Told me it wasn't right to speak to her while she was so out of sorts and to come back the next day. Once I knew you were on the way, I left her to you."

Joseph nodded. "Who did you verify was in the wood or around the scene of the crime before it happened?"

"Mr. Hadley, Mr. Smith, Mr. Evans—all sporting outdoorsy men. Mr. Lawrence, obviously with his wife, who was seen fleeing later, alone. The mousy woman, Miss Marsh, was walking with her lawyer or something like that. Bit cagey it was. They were together, however, and neither of them have any reason to try to kill Lawrence."

Joseph frowned. They also had an additional alibi through the maid who had seen them while Lawrence was likely being killed.

"Dr. Wilkes believes the deceased was killed two to three hours before he was discovered?"

Constable Daisy nodded.

"And you didn't speak to the maid to confirm the story of this Charles Aaron and the mouse?"

Constable Daisy shook his head. "They have each other alibied, no motive, and the wife was there. It's usually the spouse, isn't it?"

"Yes," Joseph replied disgustedly, "when the wife is dead."

"Goes both ways, don't it?"

"No," Joseph replied flatly. "I want you to track down the doctor and send him to me. I'll be going to the Lawrence house first. Send him to me there."

"Probably already there," the constable said. "Mrs. Wilkes and Mrs. Lawrence are good friends. They'll try to protect Mrs. Lawrence from us, despite her crime, but we'll catch her."

Joseph scowled and demanded directions to the Lawrence home. The house wasn't far, but nothing was far from any place else in villages like Bard's Crook. Joseph walked through the town, marveling how the teashop perfectly matched the book. The same pretty little lamps, the same corner placement that allowed the nosy women to watch the townsfolk go by.

He turned up the lane towards the Lawrence home, bypassing the first three houses before he came to the pretty white house with the rose garden and a white picket fence. Joseph walked up the lane, noting the curtains that flicked in the house at number seven directly next to number nine.

A maid opened the door to number nine and glanced him over. "Hello," Joseph said, "I need to speak with Mrs. Lawrence." He held out his card and the maid examined it.

Her mouth tightened, but she stepped back to let him in. Joseph was led to the parlor where a man with dark hair sat. He was smoking alone.

Joseph held out his hand. "Detective Inspector Aaron."

"Dr. Wilkes," the man said, as they shook hands.

Joseph glanced him over. "Tell me about Bertrand Lawrence."

Dr. Wilkes's mouth twitched and he glanced away, considering before he spoke. "Theodora and I married within weeks of Harriet and Bertrand. We spent quite a bit of time together in those early days when Lawrence was writing his tripe and I was building my practice. Never liked him. Not then. Not when he became successful. I hate to say it, but I don't regret him now. He spread dissension and cruelty like kind people spread happiness."

Joseph nodded, making a note. "Would you tell me about Mrs. Lawrence?"

Dr. Wilkes scrutinized Joseph carefully. "I suppose I have to answer."

"What do you mean?" Joseph asked. The doctor avoided Joseph's gaze. "Why wouldn't you answer?"

Dr. Wilkes leaned back. "Harriet is clever. She and Theodora, my wife, are good friends. If Theodora would not do a thing, then Harriet would never do it. Only," he paused, "Harriet confessed to Miss Marsh and my wife that she'd considered murdering her husband. Theodora maintains it must have been theoretical after a particularly trying day, and maybe she's right."

"Did Mrs. Lawrence experience violence at her husband's hand?"

"Ever?"

"Often?" Joseph countered. He had heard of Mrs. Lawrence's bruised face already, but Dr. Wilkes didn't know what Joseph knew about the bruise.

"Too often," Dr. Wilkes admitted. "Nothing like poor Mrs. Evans. Have you heard of the nonsense surrounding this book?"

Joseph nodded. "I have."

"That author caused more trouble than is justified by whatever he got paid."

"That author," Joseph said, thinking of the sweet Miss Marsh, "is not responsible for the crime that has been committed. Fiction or fact. Is it possible that Mr. Lawrence had a relationship with Mrs. Evans?"

Dr. Wilkes shook his head. "Mrs. Evans does nothing without the approval of her husband. There is no chance, not the slightest glimmer of an opportunity, that she would have been able to create a relationship with someone like Lawrence. And he had no interest in already defeated women like Mrs. Evans. Lawrence was a man who liked to make strong people, men or women, crumple. He liked to manipulate them into recognizing how brilliant he was."

The door to the parlor opened, and a woman with a bruise came in, along with a quite lovely blonde. The bruised woman sat carefully down. "I believe you need to speak to me? I am Harriet Lawrence."

Her gaze flicked to Joseph's while her hand lightly touched her bruise, and then she bowed her head. The other woman took Harriet's hand.

"Tell me about your day yesterday," Joseph said. "Start with the morning. With the routine things."

"Why?" the blonde woman demanded.

"It's all right, Theodora. He needs to know." The bruised woman glanced at the others. "I always get up before Bertrand. I—" Harriet took a long, shaky breath in and kept her gaze fixed on the floor. "I try

—tried—to keep an opposite schedule from him. If I get up early and he slept late, well, that's half a morning that is my own again."

Joseph didn't make notes because he knew it was hard for her to admit the truth and he wanted to give her his full attention. Harriet had a clever way to deal with the man that Miss Marsh had illustrated in her book. Charles had said that the man he'd met had been spot on accurate.

Harriet, however, was an entirely different creature than the book reflected. More of the captain of her own fate than Miss Marsh had shown Harriet to be. Was that because of the murder? Or was it because Miss Marsh had been inaccurate?

"I go for a walk in the mornings when I can. If I linger long enough, I'm not at home when he wakes and don't have to cater to him. Yet, he doesn't—didn't—pick at me about it because his books prose on and on about the benefits of fresh air and exercise."

Joseph would have laughed if this wasn't about a murder. Instead he nodded and waited for her to continue. Each statement was clearly painful as she continued. "Yesterday morning, however, Bertrand got up soon after I did. I normally spend the morning in the garden before my walk. Mr. Smith walked past with his dog as Bertrand came out, and he asked if Mr. Smith attempted to steal my affections every morning."

Harriet looked up, rage in her eyes. "As though they could be stolen, as though they belonged only to him, as though—" Harriet stilled, gathering herself before continuing more calmly. "Any capacity for affection was burned out of me. I spent my days, every single day, finding ways to avoid my husband and his petty cruelty. That has been my life for years. I don't love Mr. Smith. I didn't love my husband. If I could have fled like Eliza did in that book, I would have."

Harriet Lawrence fell quiet, but she slowly looked up at Joseph, meeting his gaze directly. "I have wanted to bash my husband over the head more times than I can count."

"Harriet!" Theodora hissed.

"But I never did. I didn't yesterday morning either. I hope that you can believe me."

"I would like to," Joseph told her gently. "I happened to be on the train with Miss Marsh, who told me in no uncertain terms that you were not the killer."

"She doesn't have the imagination to see me as anything other than a devoted wife, though I appreciate her defense. I hope that there is more to clear me of this crime than her statement."

Joseph blinked rapidly as he made a note into his book to hide his shock. This woman truly had no idea that Miss Marsh had written that book.

"Miss Marsh is not the only one who believes in you, Harriet," Theodora assured her.

"Does your husband own a cricket bat?" Joseph asked.

Harriet straightened. "Is that how Bertrand died?"

Joseph nodded once and Harriet paled. "He owned several, I think. They were in the little shed in the back garden."

"May I see them?"

Harriet nodded.

"Do you know how many he had?"

Harriet shook her head.

"Would you recognize a cricket bat as one of his if I showed it to you?"

"I've never been sporting," Harriet told them. "You could line up every cricket bat in Bard's Crook, and I would have no idea which ones belonged to Bertrand."

Joseph frowned. "Is the shed locked?"

Harriet shook her head. "We don't even lock our doors, Detective Aaron."

CHAPTER 18

CHARLES AARON, PUBLISHER

"You are a solicitor?" Miss Hallowton asked the next morning.

Charles looked up from the breakfast that she'd served. It was a simple enough meal. Eggs, fried bread, bacon, and both coffee and tea.

"No," Charles hedged, trying for a charming grin. "I work for a company in London."

"That handles some sort of beneficiary or—ah—something for Miss Marsh."

Charles sipped his coffee before he answered. "I'm afraid the nature of my work is confidential."

"So Miss Marsh didn't inherit something?"

Charles pretended to consider. "She came into a recent good fortune of which I am here to assist."

Miss Hallowton refilled his coffee and then seated herself. "I've always liked Miss Marsh. She's timely in returning her books to the library, and they come back in excellent condition."

Charles nodded once and finished his coffee quickly. It was as though Miss Hallowton had never met Miss Marsh at all if the only thing of note to say about the quiet author was that she returned books? Charles would have chuckled to himself if he didn't see in the librarian a woman that Miss Marsh seemed to like. She'd given the woman an inheritance and an adventure in her book.

In the second book, the librarian had returned to Bard's Crook with a handsome, bookish husband, and the two were side characters around which Charles's own fictional persona had spent rather a lot of time.

He rose, thanked Miss Hallowton for her meal and exited the cottage. On the way out, he found Mr. Hadley approaching the door.

"Good morning, Mr. Hadley. Any news?"

Hadley shook Charles's hand. "The yard man is on the way."

Charles placed his case in his auto and motored to Miss Marsh's house, hoping that it would be Joseph who was assigned to the case and that his nephew had thought to bring Charles a change of clothes.

Charles left the auto outside of Miss Marsh's charming little cottage. He believed she would agree to his intruding to use her home as a base. Eunice opened the door, examined him carefully, and then stepped back.

"Miss Marsh said you'd likely come by," Eunice said. "She's gone to London with that sassy Miss Marian Parker, but she said she'd come back as soon as they were done."

Charles went into the parlor as directed, using the desk there to make notes on the manuscript. He worked through the morning and found a plate of sandwiches and coffee at his elbow as he started on a letter to the author who had requested a larger advance.

It was just before tea when the door opened and Georgette appeared. The puppies in the kitchen barked the moment Georgette called to Eunice.

She glanced into the parlor. "Oh, Charles! I do hope you'll forgive me for abandoning you." She placed her parcels on the small table and removed her coat.

He felt both as though he was seeing a stranger and also that he was seeing quite his favourite person and seemed to have lost the ability to speak. He noticed the delicate lines of her rounded face. The healthy glow to her skin. The way her eyes were both quiet and shining, but always sweet. It seemed as though you had to earn her trust to see that shine in her gaze, which made him enjoy it all the more.

With a dress that fit her, however, it was possible to see her trim figure and swan-like neck. With a deep green jumper over a blouse and pleated skirt, he could see the variation of color in her hair, the creaminess to her skin under her freckles.

She was not and would never be a great beauty, but when adding her clever mind to her appealing face, she was quite attractive, especially with that charming smile.

"Why, hello there," he said. "You are completely forgiven seeing as how I have thrust myself onto your home and into your life. I appreciate your Eunice taking such good care of me. May I say what a charming ensemble that is?"

"You may." She grinned and then a flash of humor crossed her gaze, and he realized that she was comfortable enough with him to let him see it. "May I say what a charming nephew you have? I believe he is quite taken with Miss Parker."

Charles paused, having to switch gears in his mind. "They sent Joseph then?"

"I recognized him on the train." Georgette laid her coat on the table and topped it with her cloche. He was pleased to see they were both new and that she'd spent some of her advance for the new book on herself. "You have the same—" She pointed to her chin where his cleft was and then trailed off before she added, "The same eyes as well. The same build. You could be his brother rather than his uncle."

Charles laughed as he seated her in the parlor. "Well, I am not so much older than him. I was quite the surprise to my parents."

GEORGETTE MARSH, SECRET AUTHOR

Charles Aaron stayed with Georgette through tea and had returned to the report he was writing for his partner while Miss Marsh worked on her book. It was then that the congeniality of the afternoon occurred to her. This must be what it is like, she thought, to have friends. With Marian and Charles, Georgette didn't feel the need to hide who she truly was, nor did she feel the need to pretend to something she was not.

She was a good dozen pages into her third book when Detective Aaron arrived at the cottage with Marian Parker right behind him.

"Hello," Marian said, holding out her hand to Charles. "You're the brilliant man who saw past Georgette's clever mask. My Aunt Parker doesn't believe me when I tell her how clever I think Miss Marsh is."

"I'm not surprised after the conversation I just had." Detective Joseph Aaron shook his head in irritation, and Charles lifted a brow.

"They see what they want to see." Georgette glanced among them.

"But why?" Marian demanded. She was a most gregarious young woman and was entirely unafraid to ask the question that the others avoided.

Georgette nibbled at her bottom lip and then decided if she wanted true friendships of the like she was hoping would grow between herself, Charles, and Marian, she had to be honest. "I've always been quiet. I had a stutter when I was younger. I don't think I would have been inclined to chatter, but I definitely had no desire when it was so painful to speak. When I left for school, I eventually outgrew it, but no one I knew from here was at school."

"And after you came back?" Charles asked.

"My parents died just after. Only a few months really."

"Oh!" Marian said, perhaps feeling the pain of it since Georgette was Marian's age when it happened.

"For a long while, I didn't have anything to say."

"And when you stopped mourning, it was too late to escape their impression of you," Charles finished for her.

She nodded, fiddling with the sleeve of her new jumper. "It didn't help that Eunice and I couldn't afford much. We have been rather painfully poor for a while, and people do care so much for appearances. They can't imagine me as anything other than a dowdy, stuttering, slightly dim creature, and my personality doesn't lend itself to escaping how they see me."

Detective Aaron accepted a mug of the coffee that Eunice brought. "I hope you don't mind if I ask you to stay," he said to Eunice. "From what I understand from Miss Marsh, you may have some details to help me understand what has been happening here."

"I have lived here since I was a girl," Eunice declared. "One moment."

She returned twice more, once to set down a tray of sandwiches and sweets and the second with teacups and a pot of tea to go with the coffee. It seemed that Eunice had supplemented their kitchen while Georgette had been supplementing her wardrobe. Georgette didn't mind in the least, given that she was famished and cucumber sandwiches were one of her favourite things. Add poppy seed cake and a jam tart and all was right with the world.

A moment later she had to admit that the murder put a damper on things, but this was still one of the most enjoyable teas she'd had for some time.

They ate silently, lost in their own thoughts with Eunice sitting at the ready. Finally, Detective Aaron set aside his coffee, thanked Eunice and Georgette, and asked, "This Mr. Smith—you believe he has feelings for Mrs. Lawrence?"

Eunice nodded. "Normally I wouldn't be one for gossip."

"A murder makes these extraordinary circumstances," Detective Aaron said agreeably.

"Just so," Eunice said and sipped her tea. Georgette knew the move as one where Eunice was gathering her thoughts. "I was employed by Miss Marsh's parents when my girl was born. Or soon after, as to be of little difference. At the time, the other nurses and I interacted rather a lot. They were looking after Harriet, Theodora, Bertrand, Melvin, and soon enough Eliza, though she's just a touch younger than Miss Georgie."

"Who is Melvin?"

"Mr. Smith," Eunice said. "Bertrand was always a little blighter. Melvin always followed around little Harriet. He was in love with her from the time he was in short pants. He never wavered."

"So your assumptions are based off of those days?" Detective Aaron sounded hesitant and Eunice clucked at him.

"It's more than that." Eunice glanced at Georgette and then back at the others. "It started then. It never stopped."

"Eventually he married and she married. Other people."

"Mrs. Smith knew he was in love with Harriet Lawrence. It came up every time they had a disagreement. Since Mrs. Smith passed away, Melvin Smith returned to outright lurking around Harriet Lawrence."

Detective Aaron wrote a few notes in his notebook while Charles sipped his coffee and Marian hung on every word.

"Do you think that Melvin Smith is capable of murder?"

Eunice shook her head. "I won't be part of that. I'll give you what I know, but I don't feel right about guessing who might be a killer."

Detective Aaron nodded and Georgette wondered.

"Who do you think killed him?" Marian asked Detective Aaron.

His gaze warmed while he looked her direction. "I have to keep my thoughts to myself."

Marian turned to Georgette and asked the same question.

"I don't want it to be Harriet," Georgette admitted. "Of the two who I think are most likely—Mr. Evans and Mr. Smith—I would prefer it to be Mr. Evans."

"Why?" Detective Aaron demanded.

"His daughters," Georgette said simply. "It would be terrible to be the daughter of a murderer, but perhaps better than to be constantly tormented by him. Mr. Smith isn't a devoted father, but he isn't cruel."

"Those little girls are poor mites," Eunice agreed. "Mr. Evans has a heavy hand and a tyrannical eye."

CHAPTER 19

JOSEPH AARON, DETECTIVE INSPECTOR

"I'd like to speak with Mr. Melvin Smith, please," Detective Aaron said to the maid at the small brick house near the edge of the wood.

According to Eunice and Harriet, Mr. Smith walked past the Lawrence house nearly every fine day. Although Bard's Crook wasn't a large village, that house was on the opposite end of the village and the poorer walk. If the man simply turned to the right instead of the left, he'd be rambling through a wood.

Joseph shook his head as he was taken to Mr. Smith's office. After he was seated and coffee was brought in, Mr. Smith cleared his throat. "I hope you don't believe Mrs. Lawrence killed her husband like that fool Constable Daisy."

Joseph saw the fervor in Smith's gaze that proclaimed the love that Eunice was certain the man felt. Joseph wasn't sure he disagreed, seeing that nearly mad look in Smith's gaze. The question was: did he love her so much he killed her husband?

"Miss Marsh told me the same thing," Joseph said, unable to help himself in seeing another view of Georgette Marsh.

Mr. Smith frowned and then scoffed. "Wouldn't have thought Miss *Marsh* would have been so discerning. I'll have to compliment her."

Detective Aaron cleared his throat and pulled out his notebook. These fools really had no idea that Georgette Marsh, the quiet, one-time stutterer, had been the one to unveil their secrets in her book.

"I need you to describe the day of Mr. Lawrence's death for me. Start with when you woke, please."

Mr. Smith cleared his throat and leaned back. The expression on his face didn't lend to confidence in what the man was about to say. He was fidgeting and avoiding Joseph's gaze. "Always have been an early riser. Got up and did some business, took care of some letters and such. Then I had breakfast. It's always precisely at 8:00 a.m. Always the same as well. I tend to be a man of routine. Porridge, sausages, eggs, and fried tomatoes. After which I went on my walk."

Joseph made sure to look up from his notes as he asked, "Where do you walk?"

Mr. Smith looked Joseph directly in the eye as he answered. "Walked in the wood. Would have thought that would have been obvious since you've heard that I witnessed Hadley in the wood that day as well."

Joseph lifted a brow and made a slow note in the book, waiting until Smith shifted uncomfortably before he looked back up and asked, "And do you often walk in the wood?"

"It's right there, isn't it. Walk there often enough."

Joseph leaned back, meeting Mr. Smith's gaze. "But you said that you're a man of routine. So that walk is your routine walk?"

Smith flushed and cleared his throat again, fingers fidgeting. "Sometimes I walk towards town."

"Most days," Joseph clarified and waited for Smith to nod. "Most days, in fact, you walk past Mrs. Lawrence's home and ensure that you have a few minutes to speak with her."

Smith was a brilliant red and his eyes were wild as he ground out, "There's no crime in walking in the wood or walking in the town."

Joseph used that smooth voice that his uncle had taught him. It was precision and calmness in the face of another's anger that often made you their master. "Indeed, where you walk your dog is not a crime. It is, however, a telling point that you spent so much time chasing after the victim's wife."

Smith thrust himself out of his chair, turning on the detective. "What of it? What if I say hello to an old friend every day. Did Miss Marsh send you my way?"

Joseph scoffed. "Miss *Marsh?* I assure you the quiet little woman is not leading this investigation, the facts are. And the fact is that you spent quite a bit of time chasing the victim's wife. The fact is that you were in the wood on the day of the murder—an unusual decision for you. The fact is that Mr. Lawrence laid hands on his wife and she fled the man. Did you act?"

Smith had paled, but his ears and cheeks were still dark red while the rest of him looked ill. "Laid hands on her?"

"You knew, didn't you? That Mr. Lawrence could be a violent man?"

"That's Evans," Smith countered, sounding almost sick.

Was the man acting, Joseph wondered, or did he really not know? "So I understand. Mr. Evans is known to be violent. Mr. Lawrence, however, was secretly violent."

Smith blinked rapidly, gaping like a fish, and then he breathed out darkly, "That fiend."

"Come now," Joseph said, "come now. You knew. Mrs. Wilkes knew. Dr. Wilkes. Mrs. Lawrence's servants. I believe that Mr. Lawrence even suggested that a man keep his wife in line in his books. Didn't he?"

"He doesn't—didn't—actually live that tripe he preached." Mr. Smith seemed to melt back into his seat, shuddering as he met Joseph's gaze. "Did he really hurt her?"

"I saw the evidence myself," Joseph replied, watching Smith turn green. The man was something of a rainbow of colors during the course of this interview. "Who else did you see in the wood?"

"Hadley. The Lawrences. He was with her, so I didn't approach. *Bertrand* and I weren't fans of each other."

"Indeed?" Joseph asked.

"Everyone will tell you that." Smith placed his hand on his forehead and shook. "Why didn't she tell me? I would have helped her."

Joseph didn't answer that question, but he thought he might know the answer. The last thing Harriet Lawrence wanted was to end up suffocated by another man. That was a woman who needed to breathe without a man pressing his wants and expectations on her and perhaps recover from what she'd been through.

GEORGETTE MARSH, SECRET AUTHOR

On the following morning, Georgette waited for Mr. Aaron to arrive, hoping he'd join her in an adventure. She was a little afraid to do it entirely by herself. Mr. Aaron had said he'd stay until the murderer was caught. She wasn't sure when she'd been more grateful.

Georgette played with the puppies and then worked on her book until he arrived with his auto. "Hullo."

He paused for a moment. "This is a new expression for you."

She nibbled her bottom lip, tucking her hair behind her ear. "I—"

His gaze moved over her. "Is that mischief I see?"

"I—think it might be—" She grinned, biting at her bottom lip.

"What would you like to do?"

"Something that makes me a little afraid to do alone."

"I can be easily persuaded with a cup of that delightful tea you've been serving."

Georgette led him to the dining room and then asked Eunice for some tea. For the first time, she had someone to talk to about her book, and she loved it. She told him her idea for Chester Alvin, who had become his own character now, but it seemed that Charles felt proprietary towards the fictional version of himself and voiced his opinions until she held up her hands in surrender.

"Where are we going?" Charles asked.

"The village to the south. It's not a long drive, but it's where Mr. Evans sent his wife. She's with her parents."

"Are you interfering in a murder investigation, Miss Marsh?"

She pressed her lips together to hide her grin. "I'm only wanting to visit a friend."

Charles led Georgette to the car and seated her. On the way to the next village, he asked, "Do you expect to be welcome?"

Georgette shook her head and then quietly admitted, "I feel responsible for Lawrence's death. I would feel worse if Harriet ends up paying for the crime."

"Are you so convinced she didn't do it?"

Georgette nodded, staring out the window as they motored down the road. The main square of the village was where they stopped for Georgette to step into the post office to learn where the Smiths lived. Only a few minutes later and Charles was leaving her at the Smith house and motoring down to the teashop where they agreed she'd walk to meet him. She approached the door with trepidation and then knocked lightly.

Mrs. Smith opened the door and her brows rose at the sight of Georgette, but they'd lived in the same village when Georgette was a girl, so she recognized her. "Why, Georgette Marsh, as my lands!"

"Hello, Mrs. Smith," Georgette said carefully. "I was wondering if I might take a few minutes of your morning and Eliza's, too."

Mrs. Smith appeared to want to say no, and Georgette could guess why, but the woman couldn't quite turn away a girl she'd known since she was a child. Instead, she led Georgette into the parlor and seated her. Mrs. Smith left Georgette with the comment, "You so look like your mother. I did like her so much." A few minutes later, a tea tray and Eliza Evans joined them.

Eliza moved gingerly and Georgette could imagine too easily the beating she'd received to cause such care. She was a small woman, like her mother. They both had dark hair, though Mrs. Smith's was more grey than brown. With the dark eyes and fine features, Mrs. Smith was a foretelling of what Eliza would someday be, and it was not a terrible future.

What shocked Georgette was that Eliza had been with her parents for at least a week and yet she still moved so carefully. How badly had Eliza been hurt when Mr. Evans left her for a visit?

Georgette and Eliza both received a cup of tea. "I'm surprised you remember how I like my tea."

"You drink it like my granddaughters," Mrs. Smith said with a grin. "Milky and sweet. How can we help you, Georgette?"

"Have you heard of Mr. Lawrence's death?" Georgette asked gently.

The two women's gazes met and then returned to Georgette. Mrs. Smith was the one who answered. "A tragedy."

Eliza sipped from her teacup as she stared at the floor.

Georgette took a breath and channeled the heroine she wished she was rather than the quiet woman she knew herself to be. "I think we would all agree that one less abusive husband is less of a tragedy than many another death."

Eliza did not move. Mrs. Smith choked on her tea. Georgette waited until Mrs. Smith was done coughing before she added, "What seems to be the great tragedy to me is that Harriet Lawrence is the main suspect in this crime. As though poor Harriet were capable of beating down a man with a cricket bat."

CHAPTER 20

JOSEPH AARON, DETECTIVE INSPECTOR

*T*he hunt for Mr. Evans was as successful as a snake hunt in Ireland. The man was wily, it seemed. Detective Aaron went to his home, the pub, the local police station, and through the wood and wasn't able to find him. When evening came, Joseph returned to the Marsh cottage. There was something about the place that made it seem as though he were going home for dinner, even though the time had long since passed when he'd had a home.

Eunice opened the door and shook her head. "Georgette and Charles are waiting for you in the parlor. They were hoping you'd come for dinner if you had time."

Joseph grinned and went inside the parlor, finding the two of them sitting together on a new Chesterfield. "What's all this?"

"Your uncle paid me for my second book before he had even read it. In the haze of shock, I bought furniture. It was delivered while we were down south."

Joseph took in the room. "You know? Another book, a little paint, a new rug. I can see it now."

Georgette laughed. "That is on my wish list. After Charles bought my first book I made a list of things Eunice and I needed. Painting the cottage and the fence is one of many."

"So—" Charles looked at Georgette, who blushed brilliantly.

"I—"

Joseph glanced between the two of them. "How did I become the parent here? I feel as though you two have been into mischief and I'm going to have to reprimand you severely."

Georgette glanced away and Joseph felt certain that she was debating lying. But she didn't. She said, "I went to see Eliza Evans—"

Joseph's brows lifted, but he realized that Georgette may well have gotten information that was impossible for him to acquire on his own. She bit down hard on her bottom lip before her eyes welled with tears. Her voice, however, was steady. "Mr. Evans beat his wife rather horribly looking for a confession of her guilt with Mr. Lawrence." It was then that her voice cracked, but she pulled her emotions in. "Mr. Evans left his wife and his daughters with her parents to keep her away from the gossip around the book and ideas about Mr. Lawrence. Her parents hadn't realized how bad things were for her. And—" Her mouth twisted and she had to try several times before she added, "Her parents are helping her now."

"Does that mean she's leaving her husband?"

Georgette nodded. "She's fleeing. She told me that she read *The Chronicles of Harper's Bend* and it gave her the power to leave him. She read it and imagined what it might be to live without him, and when she was safe with her parents, she asked to stay. That was when her mother started crying and said that the author had freed her daughter." Her voice choked on the last part.

"Does Mr. Evans know that his wife is leaving him?"

Georgette nodded. "He comes every day. He came while I was there and shouted outside until Mr. Smith, her father, ran him off. They've got a dog, one of those big terrifying ones, and they set it on him the moment he starts screaming outside of the house."

"Oh my," Joseph said.

"The local constable watches for his auto to come into town also. Once they set the dog on him, the constable runs him off."

"That's quite the motive for murder," Joseph said. "I can imagine Mrs. Lawrence killing her husband, but I can't imagine her killing him with the cricket bat. I can also see how an obsessed lover stuck as Melvin Smith would kill Mr. Lawrence if he witnessed the violence, but his reaction was pretty compelling. He's either a very good actor, or he didn't know about the abuse."

Charles leaned back. "This town has been quiet for generations. This murder didn't come out of nowhere. As much as I don't want to admit it, I think it has to be connected to the book."

"It would be nonsensical to pursue any other route first, especially given the utter lack of evidence," Joseph said. "There were no witnesses. There isn't enough with the body to narrow down if it was a man or a woman. We're talking about the natures of individuals here, and certainly, Mr. Evans seems to have one that is already violent."

"If he truly believed his wife had been stepping out with another man," Charles said, "I think it would be likely that the man would face a beating if nothing else."

"Maybe he attacked," Georgette said with a sigh, "and didn't intend to kill Mr. Lawrence." Joseph watched as she crossed her fingers together, winding them into a knot. Wherever her thoughts lay, they were not pleasant. She glanced around the parlor wistfully, looked out the window with an uncertain expression, and then determination settled over her.

"I have an idea," she announced.

~

CHARLES AARON, PUBLISHER

"No," Charles said. "No. Goodness, no. It's not safe."

"It could work." Joseph sounded reluctant, but he also had a strange expression as he watched his uncle. Charles was certain he didn't want to know where his nephew's thoughts had taken him.

He turned his attention back to Georgette, and his concern redoubled with the determined look on her face. "No," he commanded. "You won't be able to live here anymore. It's barely livable for you in Bard's Crook as it is."

Another option occurred to Charles, and he panicked at the idea of taking Georgette away, of becoming life partners. His nephew may have never intended to be a long-term bachelor, but Charles had fallen into bachelorhood and become comfortable.

"She doesn't actually have to reveal herself as the author," Eunice said, as she brought the tray into the dining room. "You only have to make Mr. Evans believe that the author will be there. We could start Mr. Evans on the path to believing that it's the author's fault. The murder, the divorce, all of it, and then add in that the author is going to come and explain the whys of the book to help find the murderer."

"No," Charles said, "the publisher is going to. If we were *really* doing this, I would refuse to reveal my author, but I might come myself."

"What if we have the *publisher* come but use a Scotland Yard detective?" Joseph said.

"I don't want to be left out," Georgette said, as Eunice served the food. "This comes back to how I wrote my book. Even if I'm not ultimately responsible, what I did has caused sadness and discontent and upset and I need to exorcise that. I need to clear it from my conscience."

Charles shook his head, pushing himself from the table. "We're discussing taunting a possible murderer."

"We are," Joseph said. "I would think that they would recognize that this was a trap. We need it to seem natural. Having only the publisher come would not be enough. They would expect the author. Now," Joseph sat back, decided, "how do we begin the rumors?"

Eunice snorted. "The Evans's housekeeper blathers incessantly. All you need to do is make sure she knows, and he'll know."

"That would give us time to get a detective to play the part of the publisher."

"It needs to happen at a place that seems natural."

Charles rubbed his jaw. "Perhaps the library?"

"No, that puts Miss Hallowton at risk," Georgette said. "If we can get her to help, we could do it at Harriet's home. She doesn't have to be there, but if it is thought that the publisher is coming to Harriet's house *with* the author, it might work."

"The veiled and heavily disguised author," Eunice said, protectively.

"If you were to be disguised as well," Joseph told Charles. "There would be no reason to worry for Georgette. You'd be there to protect her."

"I hate this plan," Charles said. "I despise everything about it."

They ate in near silence, which ended in Charles demanding, "What are we going to do if this doesn't work? How are you going to find the killer?"

"There isn't much to go on. If the killer isn't Mr. Evans and whoever did kill Lawrence doesn't appear, what will you do?" Georgette asked.

Joseph stood and paced while Charles lit his pipe. "There isn't enough evidence to arrest Harriet Lawrence. If we don't find the killer, her life will be ruined."

"If it hasn't been already," Georgette sighed.

"Especially given Constable Daisy's attitude towards Mrs. Lawrence. He believes I should arrest her. If I am unable to find enough evidence to work from, and I'm not done trying, he will make it clear that he thought she killed her husband and eventually everyone around her will believe it as well."

Georgette covered her mouth.

Joseph turned to her. "None of this is your fault, Georgette. I can tell you don't believe me, but there were others who didn't come off well in your book. They didn't commit murder. Constable Daisy's attitude is not your fault. If Evans killed Lawrence, that isn't your fault. The good things aren't yours either. Mrs. Evans might escape because you helped her imagine it, but she's also leaving her husband and picking up the fight of divorce because she has reached her limit. That bravery comes back to her, and your words were simply what she needed to hear at the right time."

Eunice snorted. "That was a sound and well-deserved piece of humble pie."

CHAPTER 21

GEORGETTE MARSH, SECRET AUTHOR

*I*t took three days to start the rumors flying. Joseph continued to work the case, walking the banks of the stream, looking for evidence, sending local constables to search for clues in the wood, promising Georgette that there was no sign of lost or perished puppies. While he worked, Georgette and Charles continued silently working in her cottage, making strides in her book.

They waited to proceed until Georgette had heard the rumor several times as they passed the rumor of when the publisher and author was coming to town. There was so much assumption about who Charles might be to Georgette that she clammed up even more than usual, which both faded the rumors about the potential couple and allowed rumors to refocus on the murderer.

When she dressed in her old clothes, she felt as though she was putting back on skin that didn't fit. Georgette stared at herself in the mirror and laughed a little sadly. That was the version of herself she knew, the dowdier one whose skin seemed sallow against the dyed grey of the dress. Somehow she had become so comfortable so quickly with the changes that life had offered her. It was time, she thought, to recognize that no matter the color of her dress, in a veil or not, she was still Georgette Dorothy Marsh. Eunice came in with a hat that had a thick veil, and Georgette lost all vision of who she was outside of her mind.

Charles hid himself with a driver's uniform, a hat low on his head, and thick spectacles. It wasn't possible to hide the cleft in his chin, but his manner changed hugely. Together they got into his auto and drove outside of town to the rented auto that would bring her into Bard's Crook, hiding who they were.

The house was empty when they arrived except for a servant that had been replaced by a London constable.

"Are you all right, miss?" he asked, as she took a seat near the fire. Did he see her hands shaking? Did he know she was terrified? She was sick to her stomach, mind ablaze with worry, and certain that somehow she would be forced to face what she had done and lose it all, along with what little support she possessed in the village that had raised her.

"I'm fine," she lied.

They heard a rustle at the back of the house and then Mr. Thornton barged into the drawing room.

"What's all this?" he demanded, with those thundering brows. "Who are you, madam, and where is the author of that nefarious book?"

"I—" Georgette cleared her throat and then deepened her voice. "I beg your pardon, sir!"

"Here now," Charles said, trying to put on an accent, and to Georgette's ears failing terribly, but Thornton didn't seem to notice. "What's all this?"

"What's all this? What's all this?" Mr. Thornton asked. "I heard the author and that idiot publisher were coming to the village, and I am determined—determined I say—to force them to account for their actions! Mocking the good people of Bard's Crook. Making myself an idiot. Making poor Mrs. Baker loose, making Eliza Evans untrue to her husband. Nefarious lies and murder! Murder, I say!"

Georgette flinched at each shout, even with Charles sidling his body in front of hers, protecting her from Thornton. Before she could reply or Thornton could get carried away again, another man appeared. This time it was Mr. Smith.

"Is this the author then? This *woman?*"

Georgette didn't even have to lie when Thornton snorted, "A woman? I might believe a woman wrote it if it were all nonsense, but I'd like to know how a woman could know my business."

"As if you don't shout it from the rooftops every time you change the will. You make a fool of yourself, man, and all the author did for you was catalogue it."

Mr. Thornton's face changed to a terrible color of red and he sputtered. Georgette took hold of Charles's hand for comfort, certain she was about to face yet another death, when Miss Hallowton sidled into the room.

"Isn't the author here yet?" She held a copy of *The Chronicles of Harper's Bend* in her hands and said quietly, "I did hope for an autograph. I collect signed books, you realize. Some people like stamps, but I like books signed by authors. Especially clever ones."

"Clever?" Mr. Smith yelled. "That book got a man murdered, my sister brought shame on our family by divorcing her husband, and it has caused no end of shame."

"But the author did tell the story so well," Miss Hallowton said. "She doesn't lose the plot in the rising action. Putting together your sister and Mrs. Lawrence as was done, it allowed the author to compare and contrast the ways in which we are tortured. Didn't you think?" She glanced at Georgette.

"I—I—I did not think," Mr. Thornton shouted.

Georgette stared at the tableau in front of her and choked. Choked, she found, on a laugh. She might not have expected to see a person reading her book, but Georgette had. She'd paid her bills with her writing. She'd given hope to the hopeless with a little imagination, but this—this had to be the first time ever an author had witnessed such madness.

"Who *are* you?" Thornton demanded of Georgette, but before she could come up with a lie, a stone was thrown through the window of the parlor, shattering the glass. Thornton yelped, dropping to his knees and covering his head.

The London constable darted out of the parlor while Mr. Smith calmly brushed the glass from his jacket. "Probably another victim of that fool book. Like this woman here. So ashamed she won't even show her face."

"Oh, I say," Miss Hallowton gasped, as Mrs. Baker slammed the door of the parlor open and marched inside. Each step was a furious tirade without a word.

"Where," Mrs. Baker demanded, "is this author? Have they not arrived yet?"

"We're still waiting," Mr. Smith told her. "Why are you here?"

"That author turned me into a loose woman in the book!" Mrs. Baker snapped. "I am here to demand my reputation be restored."

"Now, now," Mr. Smith said. "There you folks go again blaming this Jones fellow for your actions. No one made you motor about with that money-grubbing boarder staying at Miss Hallowton's."

"He did not pay in full," Miss Hallowton told the others, although everyone ignored her except Georgette, biting down hard on her bottom lip to muffle the sound of another laugh.

The constable returned with Detective Aaron, who took in the scene and cursed, causing both Mrs. Baker and Miss Hallowton to gasp and Georgette to fight against laughter a little harder.

Charles placed a quelling hand on her back, but she couldn't hold back her giggles.

"Is that woman having a fit?" Mr. Thornton demanded. "Someone slap her soundly and snap her out of it. We hardly have time for female hysterics at a time like this." His eyebrows frowned fiercely at Georgette's veiled face.

"I'm sorry," Georgette choked out, sounding like she had been weeping. Mr. Smith handed her a handkerchief, which she took quietly, pretending to dab at her tears. Oh, she thought, she did live in a town full of the most self-centered fools in the whole of England.

This was certainly going to end up in the next book, Georgette thought. The sheer lunacy of the moment demanded to be immortalized. She looked towards Joseph, who scowled at the group of Bard's Crook neighbors sniping at each other as they waited for an author to appear who they should have realized was the veiled woman in their midst. She could read his thoughts easily— Were they really such fools?

The door slammed open again, and both Charles and Georgette turned, Charles with resignation, Georgette with eagerness, both expecting to see another person angry at their portrayal in the book, when Miss Hallowton screamed and fainted.

"Oh please," Mrs. Baker said, as she stared at Mr. Evans, ignoring the gun in his hand. "What are you here for? To murder the author for showing you are a terrible husband? We *all know*, Evans. It's why no one likes you. Though I think your Eliza will regret losing you when she has to pay her own bills. They're quite inconvenient."

Mr. Evans's wild gaze darted about the room. "Shut up! Where is the author?"

"He's not here, yet," Mrs. Baker said witheringly.

"Put the gun away, Evans," Mr. Thornton insisted. "People will think you killed Lawrence if you keep up this idiocy."

"He stole my wife's heart!" Mr. Evans shouted at Thornton. "Lawrence ruined my family. Everything is his fault. His and Jones. They're both going to pay. I won't rest until they both do."

"What are you going to do then?" Mrs. Baker demanded. "Kill the rest of us? Put your gun away before someone gets hurt."

"That's enough of that now, my brother," Mr. Smith told Evans. "Eliza will get over it, and all will go back to normal. It's not like more than one man hasn't had to settle his wife down upon occasion."

Evans's answer was to crack Mr. Smith over the back of the head with the pistol, and the man dropped to the ground. "Anyone else?" He gestured with the pistol haphazardly.

Georgette dug her nails into Charles's wrist as she reached slowly to take hold of the fireplace poker next to the hearth. She rose to her feet. Mr. Evans was facing the broken window, staring down the lane.

"Get over it? She told me she hates me," Evans shouted at the room. "Eliza told me she regretted the day she married more than any day except that of her birth. She told me that she would rather die than spend another night in my arms or a day under my roof." Evan's voice cracked.

The sound of a motorcar filtered through the room.

"Oh please," Mrs. Baker said, but fell silent as Evans aimed his gun towards the auto. "What if it isn't the author?" she asked. "Aren't you going to verify first? You could be killing someone's grandmother."

"Casualties of war," Evans said without regard.

"Put the gun down!" Joseph shouted at Evans, who didn't seem to hear Joseph or any of the shouting group.

There was nothing for it, Georgette thought, tightening her hand on the fireplace poker. She calmly stepped forward, lifted the poker, and smashed it over the back of Evans's turned head.

"Hear, hear," Mrs. Baker applauded. "Seems he deserved that for Lawrence. Leave it to a woman to do the dirty work while the men sit about and try to chat it out."

Georgette dropped the poker and turned into Charles's sudden embrace while the room erupted into chaos. Joseph took hold of Charles's shoulder. "Get her out of here."

A moment later, Charles lifted her and took her out the back of the house.

"I can walk," she told him.

"I feel better with you here," he replied, clutching her close.

"Well, it is a novel sensation," she told him, blushing, though he couldn't see it through the veil. "It seems I am getting all sorts of fodder for my next book."

CHAPTER 22

GEORGETTE MARSH, SECRET AUTHOR

"That seems unlikely," Eunice said as they finished repeating the story to both her and Marian.

"I assure you it's true." Joseph Aaron ran his hands through his hair. "Though, I am not sure my bosses at Scotland Yard will believe me."

"It's almost as ridiculous as my girl writing a book and making so much money," Eunice said.

"That is also true," Charles told Eunice. "She does have very good fodder for her story among all of these mad people."

Marian giggled and lifted a puppy into her lap, scratching its ears as her gaze met Joseph's. Sparks seemed to fly between them.

Georgette placed her chin on her hand, avidly watching as her friends returned to their banter. For the very first time, she could both be quiet and be a part of things. It seemed that despite her old clothes, everyone saw her. And they had found the killer with their ridiculous plan as well.

"We should have known," Eunice announced, pouring tea for

everyone since Georgette hadn't caught the signal to do so, lost in her thoughts as she was. "It's not like we, at least, haven't lived here all this time. We know what they're like."

Marian laughed into her teacup and followed Georgette's silent application of too much cream and too much sugar before stirring.

"To the most ridiculous neighbors," Marian said. "May they never disappoint."

"And the most wonderful friends," Georgette added quietly, "who definitely didn't disappoint."

The End

Hullo, my friends, I have so much gratitude for you reading my books. Almost as wonderful as giving me a chance are reviews, and indie folks, like myself, need them desperately! If you wouldn't mind, I would be so grateful for a review.

THE SEQUEL TO THIS BOOK, *Death Witnessed* it out now!

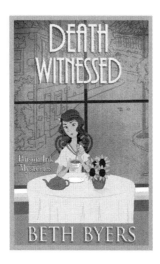

October 1936

Georgette Dorothy Marsh published a book when she was no longer able to afford cream for her tea. Without enough imagination to tell a story on her own, she wrote about her neighbors instead. Only her book became a best seller and her village was ready to take up arms.

She never expected the money let alone the results. One man died just after publication. After a pot of lapsang souchong at the local tea room, Miss Marsh witnesses another murder. When Miss Marsh realizes this murder is connected to her book as well, she turns to her friend Mr. Aaron. Once again, he brings along his nephew and they are back to attempting to find the killer, ensuring that Miss Marsh isn't the next victim, and hiding the real person behind this poisoned book.

Order Here.

If you want book updates, you could follow me on Facebook.

A Cozy Little Murder

Masked Murderer

THE MYSTERIES OF SEVERINE DUNOIR

The Mystery at the Edge of Madness

The Mysterious Point of Deceit

Mystery in the Darkest Shadow

The Wicked Fringe of Mystery

THE POISON INK MYSTERIES

Death By the Book

Death Witnessed

Death by Blackmail

Death Misconstrued

Deathly Ever After

Death in the Mirror

A Merry Little Death

Death Between the Pages

Death in the Beginning

A Lonely Little Death

THE 2ND CHANCE DINER MYSTERIES

(This series is complete.)

Spaghetti, Meatballs, & Murder

Cookies & Catastrophe

Poison & Pie

Double Mocha Murder

Cinnamon Rolls & Cyanide

Tea & Temptation

Donuts & Danger

Scones & Scandal

Lemonade & Loathing

Wedding Cake & Woe

Honeymoons & Honeydew

The Pumpkin Problem

THE HETTIE & RO ADVENTURES

cowritten with Bettie Jane

(This series is complete.)

Philanderer Gone

Adventurer Gone

Holiday Gone

Aeronaut Gone

Made in the USA
Middletown, DE
25 October 2020